CLACKAMAS LITERARY REVIEW

2021
Volume XXV

Clackamas Community College
Oregon City, Oregon

CLACKAMAS LITERARY REVIEW

Managing Editor
Matthew Warren

Associate Editors

Jennifer Davis   Jack Eikrem   Ali Noman

Nicole Rosevear   Robert Shaffer   Amy Warren

Assistant Editors & Designers

Brandon Berthrong   P.H. Drost   Brian Forney

Savannah Goddard   Isabelle Hattenhauer   Foster R. Kupbens

Justin Laib   Elizabeth Marcum-Parker   Jan Moore

Suresh Oliver   Dillon M. Tschida

Cover Art

Cloud Nine by Brook Johnson

The Clackamas Literary Review is published annually at Clackamas Community College. Manuscripts are read from September 1st to December 31st. By submitting your work to *CLR*, you indicate your consent for us to publish accepted work in print and online. Issues I–XI are available through our website; issues XII–XXIV are available on our Submittable, and through your favorite online bookseller.

Clackamas Literary Review
19600 Molalla Avenue, Oregon City, Oregon 97045
ISBN: 978-1-7320333-3-7
Printed by Lightning Source
www.clackamasliteraryreview.org

CONTENTS

Editors' Note

Time is fickle.

SomeTimes it slips away too fast to grasp, silken ribbons fluttering through clenched fists; you try your best to stay still, don't move, but weeks—months—years are gone in the blink of an eye.

SomeTimes it stops and waits for you, holding your hand as you cross the busy street, allowing you to stop and savour the moment, to remember and recall all that your library of a mind holds.

SomeTimes it falls over you, a wave of prolific, unrelenting change, crashing down and leaving you to wonder, *what comes next?*

For those left adrift in Time's capricious current, welcome to the *Clackamas Literary Review*, where we dabble and deal in Time. Stop for a spell and peruse our selection.

Delight in the Time our authors spent in creating their art, just as we, the editors, have devoted our Time in collecting it for you.

So here is our gift
Take a seat, read a while
Time will wait for you.

Anniversary of Absence

Cecil Morris

Ten years ago you were and then weren't,
a shallow breath and a pause that went on and on,
a rest extended in measureless time.

Then you moved through our lives to the cadence
of kindness, the friendly neighbor bearing red flame
grapes with their hard seeds, wild asparagus,

the garden at dawn listening to first
light whisper into shadows between leaves, under trees,
inviting flowers to open, to turn,

the cool calm of the elms, the redwoods
a steady, stately presence rising among us,
the friend of quiet ears and ready smiles.

Now you are the space enclosed in flowers,
slipped between leaves, the cool behind the summer breeze,
the ocean waving away beyond the sound.

The Books on the Desk the 1st Night of Class

Geo. Staley

Last Tuesday night, the teacher said,
    halfway through class,

    "I can barely stand it.
    I hear these poems calling me:
        'Read us. Read us.'"

We heard nothing and laughed.

He held out for most the night

    ("Longer than Adam," he would later say)

    but finally read some poems
        from the books on the desk
            out loud.

This Tuesday night, upon entering class,
    I hear poems in the books on the desk call

        to everyone

        to anyone

        to me

        "Read us. Read us."

I laugh, pick up a book,
    and for the first time
        read some poems
            out loud.

    "I couldn't help myself," I say when I am done.

    "Read some more," says Eve.

So I do though
I don't know any Eve, do I?

Sawhorse

Ken Autrey

Less a horse than a stage
for my strivings,
this ungainly beam
with spraddled legs
takes my hammer's clout,
my chisel's carving
out of notches.
My saw bites through
an old dock plank
to bare rippled grain
in treated pine
like years of waves
that lapped while boats
banged and scarred
the edges but left
the inside new enough
for shorebound life.
Water to water,
dust to sawdust,
this resurrection
levels my day
and muscles my hope.

Sleep

Barry Peters

Picture a lump of coal.
Lincoln's stovepipe hat.

Something simple,
something dark

will put you to sleep,
our father tells us.

Decades later it's he
who wakes at three a.m.

replaying the mistakes
of his life in full color.

He who stumbles to the recliner,
opens *National Geographic*

and unfolds the ocean,
who squints in lamplit glare

at the basins and plains,
the shelves and trenches,

an unexplored underworld
that would scare anyone

to sleep, including,
by dawn, our father,

whatever guilt he carries
now deeply buried,

ersatz treasure
sunken in subconsciousness.

Canoeing

Wynne Hungerford

On the first hot Saturday, we went to the lake.

But my father didn't want to paddle for long.

He said, "I don't want to get too tired."

The lake was deep.

The lake was green.

His skin was pale.

He'd spent much of that winter with pneumonia and hadn't fully recovered.

I said, "How do you get stronger if you don't get tired?"

He said, "You don't. You just get weaker and weaker."

We drifted into a cove and saw a fishing line tangled in the trees. It went down into the water and there, in the deeper green, I saw the shadow of a fish hooked on the end of the line. Being tethered, the fish couldn't get very far.

I asked my father, "Would you rather be a fish or a bear?"

I chewed the line. When it snapped, the fish swam away, into the deepest green.

"It would be easier," he said, "to be a fish."

I didn't like his answer, but I was young. I didn't know what it meant to be tired. That being tired makes you want to be a fish, that being young makes you want to be a bear.

Taillights

Stephanie Striffler

All the children in the world,
and even all the parents, have gone
to bed. You and I hurtle
along the freeway, a single star
in a galaxy streaming
away from other galaxies.
Beside me you sleep, head back
and throat bare. My hands on the wheel
are cold as mirrors, and I am alone
with a distant radio voice
singsonging the story
of a lost hitchhiker.
How do you allow your eyes to close,
knowing you will awaken
to the downshifting
engine and a tide of lights
from some nameless offramp, knowing
you will slide to me
from your dream, confused
and horizonless? You never
ask anymore if I am taking
the right turn. Across the lane

another driver's eyes flicker
into mine, as if I knew
the frayed folds of the map
tucked on the inside of his door.
He signals: *I know*
myself no better at this moment
than I know you. Red taillights scatter
across the wide lanes on the hill,
every pair another life
I could have led.

Black Butterfly

Hannah Davis

You pulled plastic
wings together
forced
comb teeth
to open wide
as if in pain.

The mouth
bites
gathered strands
of auburn.

You toss
your hair up
effortlessly
but manage
to look
elegant.

Like the way
your fingers move

with
needle and thread.

The butterfly
keeps your vision
free to create
petals, leaves, and insects
with
fabric, needle, and thread.

A flow of stitches,
needlepoint dives
back into cloth
followed obediently
by thread.

Continuous movements
repeat and repeat
like the
rise
and
fall
of ribs
with each breath.

Millions of smooth clips
with clasped teeth
live in your bathroom cabinet
and a nightstand drawer.

The black butterfly
is my favorite.

I look at it
I remember
how it seemed
to float
as it hugged
your brown hair
that glowed red
in sunlight.

Before your bones
became brittle
and
your eyes began
to ache.

We foolishly blamed
pain behind your pupils
on felt flowers
on intricate needlework.

Before we knew better.

Before you no longer
had any strength
to make the butterfly
carry your hair.

Before you could barely
stand on your own.

Before your mouth
opened
with pain
as you struggled
to breathe
baring comb teeth.

Before we knew
what was breaking
you.

I have the butterfly now,
it doesn't look as
effortless
in my
thin
blonde
hair.

I compelled
the winged insect
to grasp gold locks
that dull in comparison
to waves of ruby.

The butterfly refused,
it allowed
its spine
to break

wings snapped
in two
I was never as elegant
as you.

Pills

Robert Stone

I would say that my job is unusual, rather than interesting and we don't need to go into too much detail about it here. There are just a small number of key points; the office is in London, just east of the City, I work at night, I sit doggedly at my computer and I don't have all that much to do for hours at a time. Now it would not be the thing for me to get a book out during these slack periods, even though they know I have finished my work. No one wants me to shamelessly display the fact that the company should make three or four of us redundant. But if I want to read, then I can read online and we can all pretend I am busy, which, in a way, I am. Lately I've been reading Knut Hamsun, that old Nazi, not that I let his politics bother me much. *The Secret Sorrow*. Now that story is something else. Misery, wounds, defeats. These things are not simply setbacks, wholly negative, for Hamsun. They can be gifts, material.

The atmosphere in the office is not a happy one, if not exactly unhappy either. There are those of us, of them really, who hate this job. Some take the time to bad mouth it, run it down. I say to them, well get another job then, a better one. More money, better conditions. A job less boring that will fulfil you. If you can't do that maybe it is not the job that is so bad, maybe it's you. This is the job you deserve. But in fact I don't say that. I think it to myself.

So, the office is a quiet place, very little idle chat, despite the idleness. We are all quite tired and this kind of job attracts anti-social people, not to say unfriendly ones. I sit next to this guy, half my age, who hardly ever says anything except *hello*, rarely *goodbye* and never smiles, not even to himself. Good worker though. I'm not having a pop at him. I don't really know that he would find this description of himself fair. He couldn't honestly deny that what I have said is true, but he might say there was more to it than that. He is fastidious and wretched, like me. And he has these pills, the usual kind of thing to look at, in rectangular blister packs with a foil backing. He just throws a rectangle down on his desk at the beginning of the shift and now and then he eats a pill, washing it down with a swallow from his water bottle.

I don't know what these pills are and although I've sat next to him more or less every working night for more than two years, I don't feel I can simply ask him. Does he get headaches? We all get headaches. Back ache? My back aches. Toothache maybe. Or is he actually ill? Are the pills what you might properly call medicine?

One morning he was in such a hurry to leave (he is always in a real hurry to leave) that he forgot a packet of pills and when most of the others had also gone, I had a look, naturally. Pro Plus. That was all. To keep you awake. Every chemist sells them. All my years on nights, a life-time really, and I have never tried them. I was suddenly curious. I didn't want to take one there and then because I would soon be in my bed, so I burst one out of its blister and dropped it into my top pocket, for some other time. I didn't want to take the guy's whole packet, but he would not miss one. I saw it as a gift. I did him a few favours when he was getting started.

I do get tired at work. I have been known to slip off to the lavatory just to close my eyes for ten minutes. To take the edge off it. I sit down and I fall asleep with my forehead pressed against the paper holder so it digs a great red wedge in me and I need to give it a proper rub to get rid of it before I can return to my desk. I might find this pill useful, in the future. It held a promise; let me take away your tiredness. Having a secret pill in my pocket made me feel like a spy.

So, 5:15 in the morning, still dark at this time of the year and I have to walk for about half an hour to get to the station. I do the same walk the other way in the evening of course, also in the dark. You see some things walking in a place like this at those times. It can be a bit rough. I've done the walk hundreds of times though and I've never had any real bother. I have walked to work thousands of times over the years, but the company has moved office more than once. If you drew my routes on a map of the city, what a ragged old spider's web that would make. I still see things some nights I've never seen before.

Last night there was this beggar (plenty of them every night) and he had almost prostrated himself in the middle of the pavement. It was like he was praying to Allah. One filthy hand held out, pleading for a coin. He didn't get one from me. He was wearing a red hoodie with Community Service printed on the back and matching red woollen hat. He was incredibly dirty. Lying flat out in the middle of the pavement is certainly a high risk strategy in central London on a dark evening. Plenty of people about going to clubs and pubs and coming back from normal jobs, but in London, a large proportion of those people are absolutely not looking where they are going. That beggar was a danger to himself and others. I doubt he got much, even from the people who saw him and did not fall over him. He looked in such a bad way. If you were feeling charitable I would think you would give your quid to someone who looked like he might live to spend it.

This morning I saw a bloke washing windows using a pole that must have been thirty feet long. He had no ladder. He stood in the street and was washing windows on the fourth floor with his amazing pole. Like something out of *Alice in Wonderland*. Looked like it would be hell on your arm muscles. A young man's job. I gave him a wide berth.

Most mornings during the week the streets are quiet until you get to Smithfield. The market's already surrounded by butchers' vans picking up meat. All those white-coated men, self-absorbed going about their traditional business like a masonic cult. There are halal butchers and kosher butchers and just butchers. One van I often see has Absalom & Tribe printed on the side. A name from a nineteenth century novel. That morning I saw a rat. A big brown fellow. I don't suppose it was attracted by the meat in particular, although the smell of more or less fresh blood is detectable all around the market. There are rats everywhere. It ran across my path and disappeared into its unknown verminous world.

There is a night club somewhere near Smithfield and at weekends the gutters are full of those nitrous oxide bottles. They are a bit like milk churns but with round bottoms and shinier and of course small enough to fit in the palm of your hand. They are legal if a little bit dangerous. They are used in the catering industry to aerate whipped cream and such like. You fill a balloon with the gas and inhale the gas from that and you get a high. I have never done it but you see people inhaling brazenly in the street, like they were sipping beer from a can. I could probably use some laughing gas. Sometimes I pick up one of those little silver churns. I have several of them on my table at home. I am like that. If I see something in the street that I like the look of I slip it into my pocket. I am not ashamed. I call it street treasure. You don't know what it might lead to. At one time I thought they could be crafted into some kind of costume jewellery, the material of them.

They would make a gift if you had anyone to give anything to. They are attractive objects. Once I found one of a different colour. Lilac, I think I might say, or violet. And it had writing on it; some initials and *Austria*. The only one among the hundreds I have ever seen. I suppose it had just the same stuff inside it as all the others.

What I found that morning was much more interesting. I was walking past a club called Neo or Neon which I had always assumed was a strip joint or a casino or both. The clientele are young, well-dressed and Asian from what I have seen. They don't inhale the laughing gas. They are just a touch too old for that. Neon is quite swanky but seedy at the same time and in a doorway near there was a pile of pills, perhaps tablets another person might call them. I stopped and just looked at them without touching them. They were in these bulky square cardboard boxes, at least some of them were, the boxes about the size of a CD or a bit bigger, but lots of them were broken open so you could see the blister packs with the pills in there, white, as big as coat buttons and even some of these packs were broken open and the pills just lay on the ground, a few snapped in half.

Well, street treasure. I picked up one of the boxes and one of the blister squares. I had a look around to make sure no one was watching. There was nothing written on the boxes, nothing on anything at all. Completely plain, no logo, nothing. So I put a couple in my pocket, a couple of boxes that is, which was a bit of a squeeze, and I carried on to the end of the street still half expecting someone to call out to me or slap me on the shoulder, but no one did.

At the junction was a great flock of pigeons, all looking very grey in that morning light, thirty or more birds, rising and falling, rising and falling, at the corner of the road, as though someone were beating a smoky fire with a blanket. As I got closer I saw all of this was the work of the crazy old pigeon lady. I had seen her before. She was throwing bags full of broken bread to the pigeons, which is officially discouraged by the authorities and a bit mad anyway. Like I say, I had seen her before and never taken much notice, but this time she made me do something that I can't really explain. It made me go back to that stash of pills in the doorway and pick them all up. Every single one. All of the boxes, all of the spilled blisters, even all of the loose pills lying in the dirt, even the broken ones. I didn't want anyone to have any of them except for me. I was not sharing anything. Seeing the pigeon lady made me do that and I don't know why. It might be no more than that she just gave me confidence that no one was watching apart from her.

Now, about these pills. I do know that not everyone would have picked them up. The idea would disgust a lot of people. So what was I thinking really? You might be thinking, if those pills were good for anything, whatever that might mean, why had they been thrown away? I know that there is no point in asking a question like that about an event on these streets. How do you know they had been thrown away for a start? Any one of a million things might have happened, or almost nothing at all. The past is wiped instantly away. It is beyond plausible reconstruction. You might as well look at the pattern of post holes of a Bronze Age village and try to resurrect a conversation that had been had in that place a thousand years ago. Stare into a mummy's face and ask what kind of a fellow he was. No time for that. I was going to eat these pills and see what happened.

You could say why not get them checked out, get them analysed first? *Get them analysed?* This is not *Breaking Bad*. I could get a line of poetry analysed for you if you like. Might even analyse it myself. Would that do? See where it gets you. No. I was doing this the old-fashioned way. I don't care what you think about it. To be frank, I felt those pills in my pockets and I was thrilled. Here was excitement, or the promise of it. I had something to say. I was in the news. They might at least do my poor old back some good.

Then I had a more sensible idea. A much more plausible idea, you would think. Jacko. My mate Jacko. When I say he's my mate, I think I bought him a drink once and I have bought a little bit of weed off him a couple of times, but I know the kind of character he is and I thought he could be useful to me if I played him right. So, yes, you are correct, I was nervous about this.

He was not there the first night I looked for him, but he was on the second. He was wearing a red hoodie like the Muslim beggar but it was a lot cleaner, if not exactly clean, and it didn't have Community Service written on it, it had some stupid sentence that I can't remember now. Anyway, I bought him another drink and of course he knew something was up.

I engaged him in casual friendly preliminaries about his dog or his son or something else I didn't care about until he said, "Why don't we just skip to the bit where I start giving a monkey's?"

I almost liked him for that, almost felt guilty about what I was preparing to do to him. I pushed a box across the table. He chuckled. Greedily or stupidly, I am tempted to say.

"Looks kind of eastern European," he said.

"Could be," I said.

"What do they do?"

"That depends," I said.

There is a school of thought, to which Jacko might have guessed I was alluding, which says that a drug is what you make of it. It will make an aggressive person more aggressive or a docile person even more chilled out, or a boring person, unbelievably, even more boring.

There might be something to this, but there has to be some independent material in the drug doesn't there? An active ingredient? Anyway, I wasn't alluding to that of course. I had no idea what they did. That was the point.

My strategy here was to make Jacko think that he was in on the ground floor, on the inside track. Winning, basically. What he never had been and probably never would be, especially if these pills turned out to be a bit evil. It was when I thought of that that I did have a misgiving. I realised that I might be on the brink of murdering Jacko, although I did not like to call it that. Immediately, I didn't think it was fair to call it that because I had intended to take these pills myself and I certainly wasn't doing that in a suicide bid. It wasn't like I was dropping one in his beer while he wasn't looking. That would have been difficult as Jacko rarely relaxed his grip on a beer glass until it was empty. At one point I think I had only meant to ask Jacko his opinion on these pills, but when I started to speak, what I actually did say slipped out instead. Anyway, it was too late to back out now.

"How much?"

Jacko wasn't backing out. If he had found these pills he would have taken them I was sure of that, so there you go.

"Tenner."

"Each?" Jacko looking anxious. Eyes widening spasmodically.

"Call it eight for two. Mates' rates."

If I'd given him the pills for nothing he would have smelled a rat.

So that was Jacko sorted and it all turned out to be a waste of time because I didn't see him again before I just couldn't wait any longer and decided to take the pills myself. I got eight quid out of it, but I bought him two pints to the one he got me so that left me three quid in the black.

Pills

I got to figuring that the pills must do something, must make something happen, and I really wanted something to happen. Almost anything. They could be neuter, a placebo. If so, let's get on with it. At the other end of the scale I realised that they might kill me, even hurt me so badly in a way that would be worse than killing, but somehow, I just didn't think that they would. I know that doesn't sound so clever, but I just wanted something to happen. Death would be the ultimate happening and I reckon I thought that would be too much, too melodramatic. I knew the pills could be straightforwardly poisonous, but, surely, only accidentally so. Defective and therefore poisonous. Even that would be an event. Werewolf tablets. Could just be mildly damaging. Perhaps only if you ate them all. I wondered how long you would have to wait for symptoms.

I took a deep breath. Sitting on the edge of my mattress, feeling how thin and lonely that was. I could touch all four walls in that room without getting out of bed. Surrounded now by my street treasure. These gifts. I know seriously that you should not eat such things picked up in the street. Such things should be chosen carefully. But that takes money and time and patience and I had been out of all of these things for a while. It was a terrible risk. But the greater the risks you took, the better your chances of finding something really wonderful. Isn't that how it works in the City of London? And you don't know how much I longed for something wonderful. And besides, who do you ask about these things? Whose opinion do you trust? If you take care you just get the same thing over and over again.

I busted a fresh one out of an uncrushed box and slipped it under my tongue. Pretty chalky. Tasted right and a bit out of date at the same time. I chewed it up and cracked another one out and slipped that under the tongue. Just wait. Something must happen. It had got me this far anyway. I thought again of that Fascist Hamsun and his amazing story. I wondered if I would be doing this if not for him, if not for his story found and read at random. Hamsun and pills. Given to me. This story, given to me. Surely they must do something. Go on, do something. Go on.

Bystander

Jeanine Stevens

In line at the check-out,
a four year old ahead
not whining, more of a whimper.
I notice the feet of the woman
with him, cracked heels in rubber thongs.
She says, "Shut up," lifts him
by the tuft of pale blond hair.
He seems a rag doll,
scruffy tennis shoes dangling.
I don't say anything but cringe.
She glares at me as if to say,
"Don't you dare."

Quiet now.
I read the directions on the oatmeal box.
What did he want? Maybe he felt
ill, just asked a question?
All stored away, nothing forgotten,
he must be twenty by now.
I see him everywhere.

Ava and I by the Schoolyard

Anannya Uberoi

The children grow different now: they walk around casually
　　　　with tea roses in their pockets and music pods in their ears,
reciting words from overheard teacher-talk or whispered
　　　　by slip of the tongue, oblivious of their fluid limbs
that frisk over funnels and skipped rope, legs gliding
　　　　grasshopper-like over green football fields, stopping
only for water by the springs of the orange orchard,
　　　　scoffing only upon the grumpy ones, who like cats,
chalk in mouth, pounce and growl over pages of undone
　　　　homework.

But we grew up quiet, Ava, even as the evening
　　　　would come, cat-footed, dodging clusters of ginger buds
and trumpet-vine with restful feet. We still linger after,
　　　　fingers to the lips, plucking gossamer-winged butterflies off
ironweed, collecting wind stamped pebbles in cloth-necked jars
　　　　of bumblebee glass because we like painting funny faces
on them by the schoolyard after lunch.

We swing each other higher and higher
　　　　until the cable begins to wobble
or the bright July sun blocks the tips of our twitched eyes.

A Wolf's Reply to the U.S. Census

Geoff Polk

I was a wild child
    raised by wolves

They wanted me to be a lawyer
but I had my eyes on the deep woods.

The first day of school was hard
    the seats didn't fit
so I howled like a wolf
should.

To make me stop
    they tied me to a tree
with infinite love.

That really confused me
but it was okay—
I made friends with the other
    bad wolves

We plotted, we developed that lean, hungry look
Oh we had fun—

We smoked some plants and saw God—
she played New Orleans piano
    with a left hand to die for

We spent years trying to get
    that hard groove down.

I guess our education suffered—
they fed us junk food
    some kind of experiment
so we all ended up working at 7-11...

Did you ever get your nose broken by a junkie with a gun?
I recognized the look in his eyes
    I felt it
before the store went black

When I got back from the hospital
it was okay, except
I forgot what her eyes looked like—
    the piano player's.

For days I watched the sun
lick ice off the windows, sad and thirsty.

I had a dream, I went down to the river
with a news anchor
    yeah, she looked good
but then I saw my reflection in the water

and it was a strange creature
     not a wolf at all

So I ran and ran
until my 20's were over
     all the time thinking

I'm alive I'm alive
Oh it hurt.

Things are better now.
The woman who delivers ice cream,
I watch how she handles it
     so gently

She taught me that love is silly, infinite
     and man-made.

Imagine.

Except for her
I'm alone
     with my wild love,

my pride and evil ways.

Every day I remember the eyes
    of the junkie
    and the piano player

Mine are on the deep woods.

Teacup Speaking

Jeffrey Letterly

I prefer   what I'm made for—
    English Breakfast
    or Oolong.

        Earl Grey, if I have a choice.

I'll even take   a body full of tap water
    if it means
    you'll still touch

        your lips to me.

I'm not picky   about age or dryness or cracks—
    lips are lips,
    men's or women's

        or children's (the softest of all).

I just ask   you to not be particular
     when I chip
     from a drop

     or long-term use.

Remember   the agreement we have
     about loving
     one another

     in sickness and in health,

     in pristineness and in flaw,

     in the visible lines from being repaired,
     glue holding our gaps.

Persephone And Her Pomegranate

Cecil Morris

When our daughter Persephone returns,
she takes up smoking—Marlboro hard packs—
perhaps to disguise the pall that settles
around her, a shade in mid-day, a cloud
that fills our house and the office where she
works. She keeps a pomegranate with her,
beside her bed, on her desk, split open,
quarters gaping like a hungry mouth,
the vermilion seeds wet and translucent,
like sins waiting. We never see her touch
it, never see her eat from it, move it,
yet it looks ever fresh and her fingers
all have garnet tips, her lips cochineal.
Persephone and her pomegranate
and the dusk that follows her all day
scare us and her co-workers who wonder
if she is a curse awaiting a victim.
We fear the opiate underworld still
holds her, will still pull her away from us.

Ashtray Divers

Colton Merris

"Aren't we all, I thought, somebody's harvest?"
> —Amy Hempel, "The Harvest"

On sunny days you'd see baby ducks get pulled below the water. Negligent mother ducks would take them onto the lake when they were still too small. Blink and you would miss it. For each time you'd blink, all that would be left per peeper, per ducky, might be a ripple. The others scatter from the mother, and she would simply go on until they were gone.

Before I knew abalone wasn't said the way it was spelt, an older boy did nothing to stop a lake monster from nearly almost drowning me. Little dark hairs barely began to curl on his chest, and he was already constantly scratching at the zits that formed on his face. I was all bare, abalone smooth everywhere. We used to take turns counting how long we could hold our breaths underwater, counting *baby ducky* the way we count *Mississippi* in grade school.

Not that I could put a number to it, but I could hold my breath and swim a little more than halfway across the lake, and then a little more past that again without coming up for air. We would get in mud fights. We would dive down to the bottom of the lake and scoop up as much of the cool murk as we could. I usually knew where he was the way birds know where north is, with their magnet brains. I had a magnet for bodies in dark places and good mud.

The mud on the surface was more like silt than anything. To get the good mud, you had to dig deeper, dig past the fish poop and digested baby ducks to get a proper clod. I'd dive down, dig, and sculpt the mud into a perfect ball before swimming around to the side, clutching the black mound close to my chest.

He never knew when I came up. It's the wad of mud you don't see coming that nails you square in the mouth.

After I'd hit him, just as quickly I'd be back underwater, strafing to the other side. By the time we were finished, we'd have thick clods of the lake bottom in our hair, and the lake's algae would stink our skin. Panting heavily, he'd ask, "How do you always pop up out of nowhere?"

I said, "You've got to swim deep. When you move far below the water's surface, the top doesn't make ripples." Even in grade school I was inventing aphorisms for myself. Anymore it feels like I'm only self-plagiarizing.

There was this other game we played, we called it ashtray divers, on account of neither of us knowing what my mother's abalone shells were called. All I knew is that she used them as ashtrays and that they were oily and luminous pearl beneath the ash. We took turns standing on the deck, launching the shell into the lake while the other dove for it. The launcher kept count. One baby duck, two baby duck, three...

The first launch was the most exciting. The other boy, the one with his dark curly hairs, his muscles just burgeoning, his body just encroaching on turgid manhood, he'd curl himself around the ashtray. He twisted and coiled around it like an asp before a full release. With a snap of his wrist, the ashtray would spin out like a frisbee with cigarette butts and ash cascading in all directions.

Even if you were too busy watching him instead of the ashtray, watching the snapping arm instead of the shell, you could figure out where the shell sunk by the cigarette butts and spreading shadow it left behind. The cigarette filters bobbed, turning the green algae water around them black. Like tracing a spreading bruise or a black tongue, you find ground zero, the impact zone.

I could hold my breath for so long I usually found the shell on the first dive. My secret was to ignore the pounding in my ears, or the stars flying around my eyes. There wasn't any point in swimming with your eyes open. The algae blotted out the sun and you don't want ash from the cigarettes getting in your eyes anyway. Being underwater with my head throbbing, a galaxy spinning out in front of my eyelids, it was a place of comfort. It was an ineffable home, transient and per-manent at once like the coffin or the womb. Most important, there was purpose in the mud. You lunged your hands into the cool soft earth feeling for a very specific edge, or the smooth nacre. Back then, before I knew abalone didn't come from dinosaur snails, I truly believed they were precious as diamonds. I couldn't think otherwise, surfacing with the luminous clean shell, resplendent in the summer sun.

Holding the shell high I asked "What's my time?"

The other boy sat with his legs listing in the water, looking at nothing in particular. He said, "Don't know. Lost track of baby ducks."

I paddled back to the dock and offered up the shell. The inside was clear, luminous. All the ash had been left behind me. I climbed back onto the dock and said, "Your turn."

I threw the ashtray. My throw was awkward, the disc wobbled all over and maybe only went half the distance. Picture me, pale, hair-less, pudgy, barely able to throw. Picture him, bronze, diving, limbs thick with dark curls. He bobbed around the splash site. Each time he's down there he surfaces back a little sooner. I had counted so many baby ducks, I might have been able to start a duck farm.

Finally, he surfaced and said, "Dude. I can't find it."

"What do you mean you can't find it?"

"Like it's sunk or something."

The shell was my mother's ashtray. It was fundamental to her nightly and morning routines. She lounged on a leather-backed chair on the back porch in a bathrobe, taking long Hollywood drags. Carefully, she'd tap the cigarette into the shell. No matter the wind, not a single flake of ash clung to her. She looked like an oil painting, the sharp flat edge of her nails—Italian lady nails—tapping the cigarette. Another oil painting would be her scooping out my eyes with those fingers if I didn't find her tray. Better yet, like a Norman Rockwell, one of her ashing in my hollowed out head.

I dove in and swam out to where I had thrown the shell. The other boy and I dove against each other. We bumped our heads and slapped each other's palms, just getting in the way of each other. The big fear was with each dive, we buried the shell a little deeper. Our hands slid over the mud, tossing it in the water before it came back down and buried the shell deeper.

The other boy burst from the water, coughing and clung to me. "I'm tired," he said. "I can't keep looking for the shell." His arms and chest pressed down on my shoulders. His skin felt hard, and cool to the touch. He was like a ken doll, but with body hair. I remember how feebly he tried to tread water with his legs and his kicks kept connecting with my Pokeball shorts, dragging them down around my fat hairless ass. I had one arm trying to pull my shorts back up, while my other was somewhere between getting the older boy off me and trying to tread water. Like I was going to drown. His skinny hips kept bucking against me while he splashed, getting cigarette lake water in my eyes and mouth. I tasted algae and burnt carbon.

Somewhere above us, an osprey circled. It scanned the waters for prey. It must have been watching us, splashing and shouting. We were, no doubt, scaring its harvest with a large swath of inky darkness pulsing from our bodies. Skin. Friction. Water.

The boy eventually let me go. He treaded water and gasped. He said, "Sorry. Let's try for it one last time."

The sun was just setting. It cast deep shadows from the trees. They reached out across the lake like dark teeth closing around us. As far as the sinking ducklings and swooped carped were concerned, this lake was a giant mouth. Count all the baby ducks and close your eyes and this still won't be over soon enough. Like even after a carp swallows a cigarette and a bird eats the carp and regurgitates it to its babies. It always goes on after the fact. Even after my mother quit smoking, she still had the cough.

I had gone under. My arms dug in the mud. I knocked against a leg, then it against me. There was knee, then thigh. Something grabbed my shoulders, then my head.

Sometimes when I swam alone at night, something would brush by me. Something smooth and cool and slick, like a big worm would slap my calf or my foot. Back then, with the baby ducks disappearing, if you looked out on the lake you'd see a shadow lurking beneath the surface. This was before I knew abalone shells didn't come from extinct dinosaur snails. Must've been a lake monster. Some prehistoric thing dating back to when abalone snails were still alive had been living beneath all the mud, and it would reach up with slimy arms and eat the baby ducks. Must've spent most of its time sleeping, and when it snored or stirred churned the mud—made it good.

Must've been we woke it up, diving for the shell. I knocked against knees and shins, but this thing must have slipped past the older boy and gotten a hold of me. It had me by the head, and another arm, this turgid smooth thing, ken doll cool, pushed against my cheek and poked me in the eye. It prodded against my mouth and forced its way in.

Maybe the lake monster found the abalone shell. Maybe it was angry that my mother's ashtray woke it up, or worse, it was the parent of the dinosaur snail. Maybe it was pissed about all the cigarettes and ashes we threw into its home. For any of these reasons, it was trying to kill me.

Instead of biting, all I could was count baby ducks. This must have been the way each baby duck felt when they were pulled under water, so far under that they don't make any ripples. Pulled under like I was, like the baby ducks, the worst thing you can do is panic. Start gulping for air and you're finished. Start gulping for air and all you get is algae, ashes, and fish poop. All this starts filling your lungs and your donzo the way carp pulled from the water by osprey are donzo.

So you hope the lake monster will realize that your fat featherless body belongs to a little boy and not one of its natural food groups. You stay down there and close your eyes and count baby ducks until your ears pound and you see abalone stars bursting in all directions. One baby duck. Two baby duck. Three...

It's the wad of mud you don't see coming that hits you square in the mouth. Even underwater I still self-plagiarized.

The lake monster squirted. Its mucus was thin and warm and not like anything. Maybe it was the lake water, maybe it was the cigarettes masking the taste. The monster had let go, and I started coughing underwater. I coughed the way my mother coughed when she looked like an oil painting. Never mind that I still didn't have the abalone shell, or how at the end of the day my mother would be turning my skull into an ashtray, or how my eyes burned and my mouth tasted algae, ash, and lake monster mucus. I burst from the dark waters the way every baby duck wished it could. All that mattered to me anymore was that I finally had air.

After I finally stopped coughing—hacking out water whitened by phlegm—I noticed the other boy was almost back to shore. But my bird magnet brain already knew that. I think I called out, said something, but he was climbing out of the water so fast his shorts fell down around his skinny ass.

A small family of ducks swam nearby. One baby duck, two baby ducks, three. And he was gone. I never did find my mom's ashtray.

My mother went out to smoke on the porch that night. She sat there in her Winnie the Pooh pajamas and bathrobe, looking at the table. "She asked, what happened to my ashtray?"

I told her about the game me and the older boy played. I lied and said, "He threw it in the water and the lake monster got it."

Mom went inside and I started to cry. I cried because she was going to come back out with a saw and my dad. Whenever I got in trouble, maybe for saying the shit word or for breaking the TV by holding a magnet up to the screen to change the colors, she would hold me down while dad beat me with his belt. I was so sure that she was going to pin me down so dad could saw my head in half. Then mom would scoop my brains out and—*voila*—new ashtray.

I put my head on the table and closed my eyes. The table had one of those baby blue tarpaulin sheets one might spread over a picnic table. It was cool and clung to my skin. I tried holding my breath to stop the sobs. I counted past the thrum in my eardrums. Counted past the abalone starbursts behind my eyelids. Counted and counted. My bird magnet brain could feel it was almost over. There was another body moving toward the table. There was a tough thud, and the distinct scratch of a lighter's flint.

It's the wad of mud you don't see coming that nails you square in the mouth. When I opened my eyes, it was all abalone. Right in front of me was mom, too close, looking like an oil painting with her cigarette and Italian fingers and abalone shell.

Maybe the lake monster pulled me into an alternate dimension, or back in time. I knew I lost the shell in the lake. That by now, the lake monster had turned the totally rare, precious dinosaur snail shell into poop and it was mixed together with the dead ducks and fish and mud. But that didn't explain how mom didn't have a shell, and then had a new one.

I asked where it came from.

"My bathroom. I have two more just like it," she said. She took a drag off her cigarette and tapped the ashes into the shell with her Italian fingernails.

"So you didn't get it back from the lake monster?" I asked.

Another drag, another tap. She said, "There's no such thing as lake monsters. And I don't want you playing that game anymore. Abalone shells as big as these don't come cheap."

I sat with mom until she finished her cigarette. Her smoking replaced the algae smell in my hair. Way out in the middle of the lake, about where I threw the shell, was the moon's reflection. It rippled just a little, as though something deep below slowly churned the mud. But even my bird magnet brain knew better than that. It felt nothing but the catfish, carp, and baby ducks beneath.

Church Lady

M. Jennings

When we heard they'd found
you drowned in your pond
I remembered your winged permanent
eyeliner nonstop talking
wild stories from a life
well lived

I didn't know
you but for the outlines
echoed in the stark obit
etched in the town paper

no dates but a picture
you wrestling a mountain
lion years ago

Church lady brought to church
by wild life perhaps
with a fondness for
red-letter words like the
carpenter you married
because he could handle a trowel

pull it steady through
the wet cement of you
drawing his initials in
at the end of a needle his homemade
tattoo your body his call
your response refrained

barmaid you earned
a living too
with a pot grow a fishing boat a real estate license
each of these enough
for one lifetime you also volunteered
for the homeless and the trafficked
keeping the congregation up to date
on things we think too little about
in our rural corner

Church lady I later heard
you'd been drinking after years
sober and I broke again
to know of your cheery suffering

I didn't know you well but
your echo remains

it has been a hard
year for us all

Grandmother

Trent Busch

Helping with arguments
when he had to
Grandfather sat the porch
mostly,

shaving the tobacco plug,
chewing sparing
but regular.

He let Grandmother
do the work,
since she would,
Somebody has to,
Grandfather saying,
All right, Mother.

Because she always
stayed on the right
of things,
from saving the cow
not calf
when it breeched,

One milker's worth
three little bulls,
to correcting
the forty-cent mistake
on the store bill—

except for once
when Grandfather
lost the big argument
she, Spare no cost,
bought the finest blue
coffin in the storeroom,

and standing beside him
on her own grave
finger down said,
That man all his life
walked, let him,
God grab his soul,
ride to Heaven
on golden wheels.

Salmon Fly

Meli Broderick Eaton

Oh
dear dragonfly
you have fallen from the sky.
slender indigo spinning
where my finger breaks the current,
your spent body finished
fighting the constant pull
of gravity and now sliding fast
down the creek where

the fall
salmon has the audacity
to try going against time.
summer fat, he lumbers
against the flow, labors to find that place
he remembers, beats himself
into red completion and loses in the end.
or does he win by starting over
did he win after all?

bodies empty
blend with battered leaves
caught in the rocks, filtering
the rapid pour as their shells give in
to flow and their tiny pieces break
free to sail on ever smaller until
one with the water, they fly into the heat
of the afternoon's copper harvest,
breathed in by the sun and

reborn as clouds

Cape Disappointment

Levi Rogers

The Pacific Northwest coast is not your usual beach experience. There's lots of wind. Evergreens. Moss. Fog. Driftwood. People wear sweatshirts, windbreakers, beanies. You can fly kites and visit tide pools, but that's still only in the summer, when it's not raining sheets. Yet the beaches of Oregon and Washington exude a sort of temperament that feels appropriate for 2020. Something desolate, austere, socially distant.

I went camping with my family at Cape Disappointment State Park the day after I lost my job, six months into the global pandemic. Our office had moved out of downtown Portland in June of 2020 and everyone began to work remotely. Yet my job was not exactly the type of job I could do remote. I worked for a coffee importer and two of my main responsibilities were to roast green coffee samples and set up cuppings (or tastings). Communally sipped cups of coffee were exactly safe anymore in the year 2020.

When we moved out of our downtown office we split the lab into two places—my bosses' garage and the basement of our CEO. I didn't feel super comfortable working in their personal spaces. Neither did they feel fully comfortable with me being there. It was all understandable in the age of COVID-19.

My job description began to fluctuate daily. My hours trickled. I could see where this was headed.

There has to be an essay here, somewhere, I thought, about losing your job and going camping at Cape Disappointment State Park the day after.

I lost my job partly due to the pandemic. I also lost my job due to depression and anxiety. I couldn't focus anymore. Couldn't pay attention to small details in the year 2020 with a toddler and a pandemic and nightly protests for justice amidst gross systemic injustice.

There has to be an essay here, somewhere, about the Black Lives Matter protests amidst a global pandemic. There has to be an essay here, somewhere, about raising a toddler in the year 2020 as elections loom, fascism creeps, and wildfires burn.

Cape Disappointment or "Kah'eese," in the Chinook language, was given it's English name by the British Trader John Meares in 1788. He was looking for the Columbia River, but somehow, missed it (I don't know how—it's huge. Maybe the mouth was so big that it looked like another bay?) and named the high rock Cape Disappointment after his mistaken impression that there was no river there. The cape lies on the southernmost edge of the Washington State coast, just north of the Columbia River from the town of Astoria, Oregon. The beaches are windy, rocky, with a forest of evergreens just a few feet inland. Sand bars abound and there is only a narrow channel through the center of the Columbia River for boats to navigate. It was here, near Astoria on the Oregon side of the river, that Lewis and Clarke established Fort Clatsop (named for the nearest neighboring tribe) in December of 1805, marking their arrival to the Pacific Ocean.

Clark's journal entry is marked as such:

Cape Disappointment at the Entrance of the Columbia River into the Great South Sea or Pacific Ocean.

Tuesday, November the 19th 1805.

The winter Lewis and Clark and the Corps of Discovery spent at Fort Clatsop was a mostly miserable experience. They were cold, wet, and (I imagine) tired after trekking across the Western frontier. If you've never been to the Oregon Coast in the winter then you must know it rains, a lot. One journals entry describes their daily life as such:

December 26th Thursday 1805:

Rained and blew hard last night, some hard Thunder. The rain continued as usial all day and wind blew hard from the S.E. Joseph fields finish a Table & 2 seats for us. We dry our wet articles and have blankets fleed, the flees are so troublesome that I have slept but little for 2 night past and we have regularly to kill them out of our blankets every day.

Lewis and Clark grew somewhat disgruntled with the native tribes in the coastal region, and at one point informed the Indians that if they tried to steal their guns they "would certainly shute them.[1]" They claimed that some of the tribes would not trade with them and even stole from them, describing the Chinook and Clatsop as friendly and peaceful but also shaggy and savage compared to more eager-to-trade tribes they'd met earlier like the Mandan and the Shoshone:

"These people the Chinooks and others residing in this neighbourhood and Speaking the same language have been very friendly to us; they appear to me a mild inoffensive people but will pilfer if they have an opportunity to do so where they conceive themselves not liable to detection.[2]"

---

[1] Devoto, Bernard. *The Journals of Lewis and Clark.* Pg 285

[2] Devoto, Bernard. *The Journals of Lewis and Clark.* Pg 299

Yet as Bernard Devoto writes of the tribe, a fringe tribe of the greater Northwest Coast culture that flourished further north: "They seem to have been declining culturally before white men first saw them but the decline was accelerated by contact with the new culture. Venereal and other new diseases had decimated them, and the maritime traders had treated them with appalling brutality.[3]"

In other words: Can you blame them for stealing?

Part of what Thomas Jefferson had commissioned Lewis and Clark and the rest of the Corps of Discovery to take on throughout their journey was to make an, "Estimate of Western Indians," (taking the names of the tribes along with their size) while they also catalogued the various flora and fauna they discovered along their journey. The Corps of Discovery would even give medals to the native tribes they encountered.

Lewis and Clark spent most of the winter at Fort Clatsop reworking their journals and working on the Estimate of Western Indians while Clarke drew, "meticulous maps that proved to be among the most valuable fruits of the expedition.[4]"

I imagine that Lewis and Clark were used to being treated as special or interesting throughout their journey and were annoyed when they no longer were. Perhaps the natives made enough trade with all of the ships coming up and down the coast that they found Lewis and Clarke's white presence irksome and unnecessary. Maybe the tribes themselves were also cold and wet and grumpy. Who knows?

There has to be an essay here, somewhere about the myth of the "United" States. How Thomas Jefferson and Corps of Discovery (which included Clarke's black slave York and also Sacajawea) first

---

[3]Devoto, Bernard. *The Journals of Lewis and Clark*. Pg 299

[4]www.history.com/this-day-in-history/lewis-and-clark-temporarily-settle-in-fort-clatsop

trotted out the ideas of Western Expansion and Manifest Destiny all those long years ago, and how it has now culminated into the racial and indigenous inequality we see today.

Ironic, how those same ideals of rugged American individualism and freedoms we hold so dearly to us, (and claim are what helped us create this nation) are the same ones now making us incapable of adapting to the modern world.

During one day of our stay at Cape Disappointment, my wife, daughter, and father and I went kayaking in Baker's Bay. My daughter sat between my legs and I had to raise my arms over her as I dipped the paddle into the cold water on either side, trying not to bonk her tiny forehead. We paddled to a small island, my father alongside of us. The wind was fierce and the current strong, even there in the bay, and we had to paddle strenuously to get back to land. My daughter leaned out at one point and tried to touch the black water with her fingertips. I had to push her back down in her bulky, yellow, Paw Patrol lifejacket. I thought of how many similar tender moments my dad must have had with me when I was two or three. How I remember none of them.

One of my youth pastors growing up was a whitewater river kayaker named Ben. He told this story once about how when you're kayaking in the river there's a chance you could enter into a hydraulic feature known as a "hole." A hole is a pocket in the river created by water flowing over an obstruction of some kind. The water then continually recirculates and folds back in on itself back upstream. "If you're ever caught in one of these underwater," he would say, "Your natural inclination is to try and paddle as hard as you can to get out. But this only keeps you stuck in the hole. What you want to do is counterintuitive. You stop paddling all together and let the current take you deeper into the water, until eventually it pushes you into the current and pops you out on the other side."

While camping and before dinner one evening, my wife and daughter and I walked down to the beach at Cape Disappointment at low tide. We walked to a rock that a couple earlier claimed had star fish. We took of our sandals and walked barefoot down the beach littered with crab shells and orange pinchers. "Shiny" my daughter called them, after the crab Tamatoa in the film *Moana*. My daughter chased the waves with her tiny, fat toddler feet, running away as the waves washed closer to her, shrieking with joy. When we made it to the rock we were surprised to actually find starfish—lots of them! And in all different colors. White and purple and orange and red starfish. Tiny tide pools of mussels and barnacles. The waves rushing up around our ankles carrying seaweed and yellow foam.

I thought of the ocean. How it will outlast us. How small we are compared to it. How it erodes rocks into sand over generations. How arrogant we have become in our relationship to nature.

There has to be an essay here, somewhere I thought. There has to be some meaning, somewhere, to be found in the year 2020. But I don't know what it is yet.

As I write this, fires burn around the state of Oregon and the sky looks like yellowish brown cigarette smoke in the day, at night like a heavy dark mist and fog. Our Air Quality Index is beyond hazardous, in the 400–500 PM2.5 range for the last five days. I have not been outside for more than a minute at a time in the last week. My dog hates me. My body hates me. I ingest food and booze like it's the end of the world.

There has to be an essay here, somewhere, I thought, about connecting our years of abuse and neglect of indigenous cultures and the way they treated the land, to the wildfires burning across the West today. How for years a combination of poor forest management, climate change, and land development has led to this point in history. Did you know that indigenous American Indians used to practice their own form of controlled burns, but were once outlawed for doing so by the federal government?: "Some Karuk fire stewards told reporters that, at one time, Indians attempting to engage in cultural burns were shot dead; later, they said, they were simply jailed. Federal land policies that supported fire suppression, commercial agriculture and forestry replaced Indigenous land management," says environmental writer Debra Utacia Krol In an article about how indigenous cultures were used to living with fire. "And with a long-term drought, hotter and drier weather due to climate change, more people moving into the woodland-urban interface and overdevelopment, wildfires grow ever more destructive and deadly.[5]"

Once again, we were not listening.

Catastrophic wildfires amidst gross systemic police injustice amidst a global pandemic. A disaster within a disaster within a disaster. A quarantine within a quarantine. A double lockdown. How do we even begin to make sense of it all?

Yet I know that I am one of the fortunate ones. I have a house to seek shelter from the smoke. I have access to healthcare even without a job, through my wife's work. I have relative privilege and resources. I do not worry about being pulled over by the police.

---

[5] www.azcentral.com/story/news/local/arizona-wildfires/2020/08/27/indigenous-leaders-say-people-need-balance-land-wildfire/5624268002/

The United States, so far, has escaped what other countries have had to deal with on a yearly basis—crippling natural and political and democratic disasters.

Perhaps our moment of reckoning has finally come. Perhaps we even deserve it.

A week ago I listened to a panel hosted by a local PDX organization my brother-in-law helps run called IMiRJ, or the Interfaith Movement for Immigrant Justice. IMiRJ hosted a Zoom forum with several local BIPOC leaders here in the area to discuss the ongoing protests in Portland and hear from people on the ground about what was actually happening. A lot of the faith community wanted to be involved in the Portland protests, but they were also frustrated by the violence happening. In short, a lot of white people wanted their lives to go back to normal and for people to protest "nicely" and with "civility." And who can blame anyone really for thinking such things in the year 2020? We all want things to go back to "normal."

But what do we mean by normal? Do we mean pre-COVID-19 normal? Or do we mean the "normal" world in which black and brown people still get shot by the police, but we white people don't have to be made uncomfortable by nightly protests?

I found what one of the leaders said to be particularly meaningful for our moment. They talked about the idea of *tension*, how most times we want to move beyond it, but sometimes it's good to stay in it.

The year 2020 has thoroughly wrecked nearly all of us. Our ego and notions of control have all been rocked at some point this year. Everything is slit open. But maybe that's the point. Maybe this is the year we are finally supposed to grieve, lament, and march.

There has to be an essay here, somewhere. Maybe it's that where we're all called to live in the tension in the year 2020. To embrace it, sit in it, refuse to return to normal, and refuse to return to our individual comforts. Maybe we need to go deeper into the current rather than fighting to return to the surface of how things were. Maybe that's the lesson. Or maybe it's the lesson of the ocean. That one day we will all be gone and the ocean will remain, and at this point, who knows what else.

Walking in the Time of COVID

Diane Averill

I move carefully
down the street where masked people
do the six-foot Corona dance,
then swirl past,
each of us waving our sad hands,
trying to reach across the distance in too-loud voices
with a "Hello," or a hesitant "Good to see you out,
you haven't been out for a while."
There are too many of us.

I swerve, take a solitary path
to the creek, full and rising. It's safe here in the woods.
Its turbulence is my peace, the rush of little waves
round rocks, the yellow and brown leaves with veins like mine
caught for a moment before they continue their journey.
I pause at soft pools, look down at their reflections,
learning to speak in water language. My fingers seek
cold water, feel the shock of joy.

Noticing a swirl like a fingerprint,
my palms turn upwards, feel rain
fall into my pores. I can touch anything—
moss, lichen, tree bark.

I walk on, round a corner in the narrow path
when a man appears—too close! I squirrel
off into fallen branches
step in muddy holes, try for distance
as he laughs, saying "Everyone is dangerous
in the woods these days"
and unmasked, walks away.

Window on the Sea

Condado, San Juan, Puerto Rico

Ricardo Pau-Llosa

Sitting on a cement battlement (circa 1942)
where American turrets once spy-glassed
for periscopes, I join the sun-red tourists
coupled in their morning dallies
across an engineer's jetty of plopped boulders.
The sea hits the rocks with the huff
of popped-open grocery bags,
parodies of distant gunfire brought home
to muffled ears. The coral chunks
and concrete rubble long ago settled
into their guardian chore so that crab
and mollusk and the green blushes
each wave jostles then combs
accept these hulks as home.
It must be so, when each wave lashes
what it feeds, spilling kegs of livid foam
through caverns fashioned by how each trunk
of crane-dropped slabs has lodged
into community. The water rushes
the canyons, platforms, windows and ramps.

The take on all this, ten feet above,
is that of artifice still. Blunt need attained,
the drive to colonize makes nature.
The salt perfume and the knitting picks
of a hurried crab amid the silvered
leaves and shells and the varnished planes
proclaim that what's been abandoned
to the living cauldron
will be redressed.

Collateral

Robert Krut

He says a prayer for the first time in years,
about the heart of the world being ripped out,

begging for a sun to fill that open-wound-
earth-core, then waits—

and that night, every manhole downtown
bursts from the pavement, flies upward

atop columns of light shot from each,
holy cylinders, luminary towers

stopping the city on sight, and the city
stands in awe, rinsed in the glow—

while he holds onto his secret at first
out of humility, until

one by one, people walk
to these great and blessed tubes,

reaching hands into their illumination,
then step fully into the light, above

the perfect circle mouth, and they
float, it seems, for a moment,

for a moment without gravity, held
by some hand of divine compassion

before dropping like so much mindless
meat to the great, gray-watered

Lethe that still moves below,
and *I'm sorry, I'm sorry.*

Portland, 1994

Francis Walsh

Frankie waited while Momma searched for her Daddy. Momma called the Silver House, the Commercial Street Pub, and the Sail Loft, and spoke to every bartender, sipping tea between her words and using her phone voice, the same voice she used when people called looking for her ("The check is in the mail, I promise"). She coiled the phone cord around her fingers as the search for Frankie's Daddy lengthened.

Frankie grew bored watching Momma on the phone and listening to Momma talk to someone who wasn't her, so Frankie rustled through the sewing supplies Momma kept in the old tin tea box with the hinged lid, first standing on her tiptoes to remove the box from the knick–knack shelf with all its individual cubbies, and then lifting the lid gingerly to avoid creaking the hinges. Frankie ignored the needles and thimbles and removed a spool of thread. She wrapped one end of the spool to a doorknob and then ran circles around the apartment, wrapping and snagging the thread around table legs and house plants and chairs, repeating the process until she had created an enormous web, at which point the thread snapped from the end of the wooden spool, prompting Frankie to turn to his Momma holler: "You're trapped!"

Momma didn't get angry. She sipped more tea, and said, "Momma has to make a few more phone calls, so why don't you go brush your teeth and then I'll tuck you in? I have to find your Daddy."

Daddy was often gone, but never really missing. Daddy was a fisherman in Portland, Maine, but he had never gone overboard and was not lost at sea; he just wasn't home. He was out. He was having a couple. Sometimeswhen Daddy was gone Frankie would sneak into Daddy's room and nest on the floor of the closet among the shoes and the boots and rifle through the hamper. Frankie would press the sleeve of one of Daddy's dirty shirts to her nose and inhale— the fabric smelled sweet and dark, like burnt toast with butter, and maybe a little sour, a note she couldn't place. Daddy always returned home eventually, but sometimes Daddy returned home scowling and would say "Not now" to any of Frankie's requests, while other times Daddy was all smiles and spun Momma around the living room, lifting her feet off the floor so the tips of her shoes grazed the arms of the couch and the rinky–dink television with the missing dial and tinfoil antennae. The two would whirl, and Daddy's voice would boom, singing a church song but changing the words to Momma's name ("Roseanna in the highest") which surprised Frankie, Daddy knowing the words, because Daddy always skipped mass, saying he had done his time as a child and now preferred to sleep in on Sundays. Sometimes when Daddy returned, he took Momma and Frankie out shopping to buy clothes and dinners of cheeseburgers and ice cream, future stomach aches that would ripple with pleasant memories of indulgence.

Mama said it all depended on the catch, or at least that was what Frankie overheard when Mama talked on the phone to her friends and used her everyday voice: "He had a good catch, and I didn't see him at all Saturday or Sunday. He left again Monday and he barely had half the money left." Frankie listened and catalogued. No one said anything to her directly.

Daddy returned later that night while Frankie was in bed. Frankie heard Momma and Daddy through the thin walls of the apartment, through the gurgling of the pipes, and Momma had said she needed a rest, and Daddy, his voice slowed to a crawl, was all promises, repeating two words: of course, of course, of course.

"Tomorrow she has a swim lesson at the YMCA. 10 a.m. Are you going to drag your butt out of bed to take her?"

And Daddy said: of course, of course, of course.

The next morning Daddy roused Frankie and carried her to the kitchen and plopped her at the table. Usually Frankie dressed before breakfast, but Daddy didn't know that, or else Frankie figured Daddy did know that and was allowing Frankie to get away with something by letting her wear her footie pajamas in the kitchen, all snug and cradled in half–sleep. Daddy poured cereal for Frankie and then sat across from the girl and sipped coffee for a moment before grimacing. Daddy turned and tossed the remnants of the cup into the sink that was right behind his chair in the kitchen of their apartment, and the coffee lurched from the mug and hung in the air for a moment before collapsing into the sink with a splash. Someday Frankie wanted to drink coffee like Daddy.

After breakfast, Daddy helped Frankie brush her teeth. This was Daddy's specialty. He claimed to have had a cavity once, but he had defeated the rascal through persistence and strong circular motions, as recommended by the American Dental Association. Daddy pressed the tube of toothpaste with his fat thumb and pointer and deposited a perfect curve of paste onto the bristles of Frankie's brush and then knelt and instructed her to open wide, working the bristles and tickling Frankie's gums. When Daddy finished, he lifted Frankie in the air and pressed gently on her belly, telling her to spit, and it was like Daddy was pulling a trigger, and Frankie giggled, toothpaste foam all around her mouth. Daddy kissed Frankie's cheek, and Frankie felt the rough stubble and smelled the sour smell and laughed some more. Setting Frankie down, Daddy groaned and pressed a hand to his lower back, and Frankie aped the movements, wanting to get the teeth brushing routine right.

"Looks like you got a sore back too, Frankie," Daddy said with a wink.

Frankie smiled, feeling she had done something right.

Next Daddy told Frankie to slip into her swimsuit and grab her towel, not knowing that Frankie usually packed her suit and changed in the locker room, but Frankie figured it was another fatherly discretion that Momma wouldn't understand. This time it was letting Frankie walk through town in her suit, showing off in bright red and traveling freely and unencumbered, even if it wasn't quite the right weather yet. Daddy wore his usual scuffed up sneakers with the worn-out treads, and faded jeans, and a t–shirt with a chest pocket where he kept his pack of Winston cigarettes. Daddy shook one out of the pack and struck a match before he and Frankie even got out the door.

"Momma says no smoking inside."

"Course Momma says you can't smoke inside, you're too young to smoke."

When Frankie first started swim lessons three weeks ago, Momma made her memorize the route to and from the YMCA, just in case. They always walked because Daddy didn't own a car. They were saving up, Momma said.

But Daddy turned left when Momma would have gone straight, and the memory of the route crumpled in Frankie's mind. She wasn't sure where they were headed. She kept moving, but Daddy walked a bit faster than Momma and Frankie fell behind and settled into a rhythm of walking and jogging and dragging the edge of her towel across the ground. The back of Daddy's head bobbed and puffed smoke, and a gap between the two grew, a span of ten or twelve sidewalk bricks, whose cracks Frankie shouldn't have been stepping on anyway, lest her Daddy's back break, although Frankie's face burned with the thought because when she had shared this concern about the cracks Momma had said, "Don't be silly, your Daddy doesn't need any help breaking his back. Besides none of that nonsense is true." But part of Frankie still believed, in the same way she believed in Santa Claus and ghosts, because if she was good then she was rewarded, and if she was scared then she knew what it was that had frightened her, and if she stepped carefully then she could help her Daddy, or at least not hurt Daddy, and so Frankie hollered for Daddy to slow down, and Daddy turned and grinned, the cigarette jutting from the corner of his lips like a crooked little exhaust pipe.

"I keep forgetting how short your legs are," Daddy said. Taking Frankie's towel, Daddy draped it over Frankie's shoulders and tied the two corners together around Frankie's neck, making a cape. Daddy said maybe the cape would make Frankie run faster, and Frankie laughed and grasped the edge of the towel and swept it in front of her body with a flourish. Daddy fingered a round, moth–bitten hole in the fabric and said, bullets, you're dodgin' bullets, Frankie.

The pair continued walking and Frankie stared at her feet, shuffling on tiptoes to avoid the cracks. Soon the bricks turned to big cement slabs and Frankie paid less attention to the cracks. The harbor came into view, and both the ocean and the sky were gray, like two flat stones, and Frankie watched men in shirtsleeves and orange rubber overalls as they coiled rope before a large trawler that occupied the stern of the boat. The hull was painted bright green and gulls circled overhead. It was the same work as Daddy's work.

Daddy stopped and told Frankie to wait, then flicked his cigarette butt into a puddle that shimmered with a gasoline rainbow. The cigarette sizzled and floated among other brown, waterlogged cigarettes.

Daddy pointed to a building on the corner with a window and a neon sign that burned with the word "OPEN." "I forgot something there last night, so let's pop in before your swim lesson, but don't tell your Momma, okay?"

Inside, the colorful curve of a jukebox punctuated the dim light. The floor was sticky, and the air was cool and laced with smoke. There were booths and a bar with stools that rose to about Frankie's chin and Daddy bent low to pick up Frankie and set her on a stool. A thin old man in a knit cap stood behind the bar, and besides Frankie and Daddy there was one other person in the bar—a lady with a big poof of curling red hair that cascaded along her shoulders. The lady smiled, and the skin around her eyes bunched, and she reminded Frankie of her Momma, and Frankie wondered if she was someone's Momma. Did she have a Frankie? The lady tilted a glass of beer toward her mouth, the yellow liquid slanting forward, and the bartender set a glass before Daddy, along with two smaller glasses, almost like Momma's thimbles. The bartender poured brown liquid in the two small glasses, and Daddy and the woman each picked one up, saluted, and gulped down the contents. They lady slapped the bar, startling Frankie. A cigarette smoldered in an ashtray full of crumpled filters.

"Hey, Joe," Daddy said, "get my girl a drink. Well, no shit she can't drink a beer, she's a kid, give her a soda or something." The bartender shook his head and placed a glass of Coke on the bar before

Frankie, and there was a little red straw swirling in the glass, and Daddy said, "Frankie, I would like you to meet Marlene, the knockout standing next to me. But don't tell your mother I said that."

Daddy winked and Marlene slouched over the bar to get a better look at Frankie.

"Your daddy has a whole lot of—you know, what do you call it—a whole lot of charm. Look out for men like that when you're old. You'll thank me," Marlene said, and then turned to Daddy. "You gonna give me a dollar to play a couple tunes or what?"

"C'mon Marlene. I paid last night."

"Yeah, and you kept putting drinks on my tab."

Daddy grumbled, reaching into the pocket of his jeans for a grubby wad of crumpled bills, and Marlene rose and walked unsteadily across the bar. She hunched, resting a forearm on the jukebox, and the lights haloed her limbs and her hair and the fringe of her cut–off jeans. She stabbed at the machine with a finger, then danced her way back to the bar, where she clapped Daddy on the back, making him wince.

"Lionel," Marlene said, and though Frankie knew her Daddy's name, it was odd hearing it from someone other than Momma. "Lionel, are you going to dance with me or what?"

"Hell, Marlene, it's too early for dancing. I bought you the songs, didn't I? Besides, I hurt my back."

"That's what happens when you get shithouse drunk and fall down," Marlene said, grabbing Daddy's hand and tugging on his arm. But Daddy remained rooted to the stool, and the first song Marlene had played faded out, so she turned to Frankie.

"How about you, Frankie? You want to dance with me?"

Frankie hesitated, swiveling in her stool, but Daddy urged Frankie to dance.

"Go on and take my place."

Frankie slid from her stool, and she started to dance in the only way she knew how: she jumped and clomped her feet on the floor, andshe wriggled her butt, and she crooked her arms and tried to catch the rhythm of the song. Marlene laughed and twirled Frankie around until she was dizzy and the soda in her belly fizzed. She stepped away from Marlene and flourished her cape, and Marlene stamped her foot and snorted like a bull.

Daddy turned to watch them, and Marlene charged Frankie, but at an angle so she could hop out of the way—it was pretend danger, something for a laugh. And they did laugh, all of them, Daddy, Frankie, Marlene, and even Joe the bartender, who refilled Frankie's glass as she clambered, red–faced, back on to the stool. Marlene sipped her beer, beads of sweat suspended on the fine hairs of her upper lip. Daddy held up two fingers and Joe the bartender poured two more short drinks, and Daddy and Marlene drank again.

Marlene reached over and massaged Daddy's shoulder.

"I could help you with your sore back if you wanted to come over."

He clapped a hand over hers but didn't remove it from his shoulder.

"You know I can't Marlene. I'll be fine. I have to bring Frankie home to her Momma. Right, Frankie?" And Frankie mumbled yes, her lips pursed around her straw, wondering what had happened to the swim lesson.

Marlene pouted and dropped her head.

"Fine but buy me some cigarettes."

And Daddy chuckled, saying, sure he could buy her a pack and that Frankie could help. Daddy stood, motioning for Frankie to follow, and Frankie took one more slurp of soda and hopped down. Daddy juggled the money in his hand and the muscles in Daddy's arm bunched, and Frankie listened to Daddy's instructions on how to operate the cigarette machine. Marlene was tapping her finger on the glass, pointing to a pack of Kool, saying that's my brand right there, refreshing, not foul like your Daddy's Winston. Daddy smoothed a bill along the edge of the cigarette machine and carefully fed it into the slot, following the paper money with some coins, and he pointed to the correct lever, and Frankie saw her reflection in the glass as she pulled the lever and the pack of Kool dropped with a clunk. Marlene squatted beside Frankie and reached her slender hand into the machine to retrieve the cigarettes, and then Marlene held up her hand for a high–five. It stung Frankie's palm, but in a pleasant way.

"Now some Winston, Frankie," Daddy said, and repeated the little smoothing ritual with the money on the edge of the machine. Frankie reached forward, confident, and gripped the lever and pulled, hearing the ka–chunk of the machine, followed by Daddy's voice yelling, "Goddamnit."

"Aw, you pulled the wrong lever," Daddy said, and smacked the backside of Frankie's head. It wasn't a hard slap, and she had felt worse on the school yard playing with other kids, but until now she had never felt like she deserved it.

"Jesus Christ, Lionel, go easy on her. It's a pack of butts."

And Daddy's face, at once knotted with anger, softened. He circled a hand on Frankie's back, and said, "Yeah, you're right, Marlene. It was an honest mistake, Frankie. And hey, maybe I'll like these ones better."

Frankie nodded, afraid to speak without crying. She wished she hadn't made the mistake. Perhaps she had ruined the day, and soon

Daddy would be gone again. Daddy took her hand, and Marlene rustled Frankie's hair and said they could dance together any time, never mind her Daddy. When they got outside a mist hung in the air. Fog had rolled in from the bay. Frankie untied the towel from around her neck and draped it over her head. She was cold in her swimsuit. Walking home with her Daddy, Frankie stared at her feet, scrunching her toes in her shoes while stepping on every crack that she passed. She knew the cracks were powerless now, that they only revealed some hollow inside herself where she had stored away a childish thought that would never sustain her, like the empty cache of a bird who grows hungry in winter while waiting for spring.

Not the Southern Hemisphere

Vivienne Popperl

This is the town where no sun shines
in December, where the air does not tingle
like champagne bubbles in our nostrils.
This is the town where the taint of chemicals
rides the wind, where church spires
skewer low hanging fog. In this town
streets are lined with snow walls
grimy from passing ploughs. This is the town
where the odor of spilled beer permeates
wood-paneled bars, where voices are drowned
by the sound of stray jazz lines
squeezed from old saxophones.

In this town we immigrants have no mother, no father, no sibling.

This is the town where on Saturdays
at the municipal sauna we undress,
uncover the dark curls on our heads,
between our legs. Here, the shapes
of our bodies, old, young, fat, thin,
are more than the not-blonde of our hair.

In this sauna, we sit naked, eyes closed,
sweating in the herbal-scented steam.
Waves of hot moisture engulf our bodies.
We groan. Steam bites our skins. We jostle
for the door after five minutes.
We burst into the enclosed courtyard, throw
our burnished heat-softened bodies
into the icy pool.

Here, at last, our eyes meet.

Corpse Meditation

Adam Day

There's no through trail,
really. The path is

the destination. Slow
comes the smoke. Sac

fungus grow
from the body. Constant

translation. Soon
the ground will freeze

and snow drifts
will bury the graves

for another winter.

On the Nile

William Heath

The headless houses of Egypt
haunt me. Sun-baked, red-brick
buildings standing by the Nile

ascend three, four, five stories
or more, top floors unfinished:
empty windows, often no roof.

Old or new, these drab structures,
browns darker than sand, eerie
sadness in blank windows,

resemble rubble-strewn ruins
of past bombardments. Yet
proud owners view vacant levels

as signs of hope. Sons will marry,
move in above them, sweep floors,
add windows, lay carpets, raise

a large family, perpetuate tradition.
In Cairo, however, a sprawl
of twenty-two million—traffic

a rugby scrum, each street
a logjam, chaotic architecture—
age-old rural practices yield

inhumane results. The *zabaleen*,
the people of the garbage—
dispirited, overwhelmed by

fields of sludge, hills of refuse—
no longer haul off the trash.
Forsaking peasant customs

that once made sense of
village life, people seek
sustenance in Islam.

From the air Cairo emits
the ghostly hue of the Sahara,
looks like a vast cemetery.

Hordes of people *have* made
homes of tombs, adding
packing crate or cardboard walls,

rusty iron roofs held down
by stones—it's called The City
of the Dead. All Egypt is a keg

of powder primed to meet
its match. In troubled dreams
I see those headless houses.

Om Land Security

Bruce Pratt

I describe Jaime as upbeat, but truth be told, she's an irrepressible and unflinching optimist. She's young—too young for me—and the young are often more hopeful than we old war horses, but even though she grew up Downwest in Slykesville—better known as Methopotamia— Jamie locates a silver lining in the foulest of black of clouds.

I met her at the Elk Club's New Year's Eve Dance, where she was waiting tables for the caterer and I was fronting my part-time, five-piece R&B Band, "Johnny and The Blue Lobsters." I sing, play some guitar and mouth harp, and handle the patter. I also handle the booking, which is pretty easy, as we only do private gigs, and don't work during prime fishing season when the other guys are tending their traps.

Most musicians hate New Year's Eve. It's amateur night, a time the drunks can make a musician's life miserable, which is why we won't take a club gig no matter how much cash they dangle in front of us at a time of the year we could each use a boost in the wallet. The Elks police their party, so we've worked it the past six years.

We arrive mid-afternoon, set up our gear so they can decorate around us, and come back at six for a sound check. At seven they feed us in the kitchen with their staff and the caterers, and at nine we hit the stage for our first of four forty-five minute sets. During our breaks they have raffles and door prize drawings and during one of those I got to talking to Jaime, who could, in strict biological terms, be my granddaughter were she not so wise an old soul.

Half an hour after the midnight toast, we did a drawn out, bluesy version of *Auld Lang Syne* during which boozy couples draped themselves on one and other and croaked along with me on the vocals they could remember.

Women found their purses and coats, guys fumbled for their car keys, and ten minutes later the cleanup and load out began. I stepped out the front door to pull my truck up and saw both of The Ragged Head Taxi Company's cabs alongside a half dozen Uber driver's vehicles, idling in the dark cold, their exhausts ghosting into the night sky.

The band mates and I loaded our gear in our trucks and went inside to get paid—three hundred each—and said our goodbyes to Johnny Finch who runs the club. On the way back out, I noticed Jamie sitting at the bar with Johnny's crew having a drink. "Hey, singer man," she said, "join us for a nightcap."

I'm fifty-six, in better-than-decent physical condition, and far more energetic than most of my peers, but even in the subdued light of the bar, I could tell that Jaime was still south of thirty which experience has taught me should have put her beyond my radar. Still, I sat down on the next stool, took up Johnny on his offer to have a few glasses of left-over champagne, and before I knew it, the sun was rising on a frigid morning and I was sitting with the woman of my youth's dreams in the cab of my truck at the beach, watching the sea smoke curling over the bay.

As the sun rose and the sea sparkled, I learned that Jamie was twenty nine, older than I'd thought, has a master's in Kinesiology from The University of New Brunswick, was working three gigs to save enough money to open up a studio and business in an old farmhouse and barn she'd inherited on the Donaldson Road. "I'm going to call it *Land Of Om Spa and Yoga Studio*, she said, "and hire two of my friends from graduate school to help run it."

"That's going to work in Ragged Head?" I said.

"Definitely," she said. "We'll do so killer well in the summer that each of us will be able to take a different month off in the winter."

"Your place the old Daigle Farm?"

"Yep, my Uncle Ronnie Daigle was my mother's brother."

"You're Bonnie's daughter?"

"I am," she said, "you know her?"

"I was a class ahead of her in school."

"You knew my Dad then, too?"

"Not well. He started working as a sternman for your grandfather when he pretty young, and I was into sports, so our paths didn't cross much."

"Were you at his funeral?"

"I was," I said. "That may have been the last time I saw your mother."

"We didn't have a funeral for her."

"No one expected what happened," I said.

Jamie settled back into her seat and hoisted her feet up on the dash. "I miss them both," she said. "Dad's heart attack made some sense. He was a big man, a heavy smoker, but Mom killing herself was nothing anybody saw coming."

I had no idea what to say. My instincts ran to the avuncular, but Jamie shifted in her seat, took my hand, and said "I read auras. You're a good person. I can feel your positive energy. Mom had that, too. That's why it makes no sense she took those pills."

Two months later, Jamie moved into my place, where I'd lived alone for the ten years since Bethany died. My lone sabbatical from my tree farm and excavation business occurred during the sixth months after her funeral when I went first to Nepal and then to Italy to find a way to recover. As, I'm sure, the only lapsed Buddhist in Ragged Head, a legacy from college, I figured I'd find my spiritual way in Nepal, then discover my mother's roots in Emilia Romagna. Neither happened, but I was able to grieve alone, something I couldn't do at home where every sea widow and good soul was hastening my demise by providing casseroles and desserts at a rate ten people couldn't consumed. I knew folks in need, but it was difficult as hell managing to regift casseroles and stews. I'd move them in my own container so I could return the one they came in, then explain to a proud family that they were doing *me* a favor by seeing that good food didn't go to waste. Awkward as it was, it felt good to know I filled more than a few kid's hungry stomachs.

First week of April two weather systems decided to battle it out for forty-eight hours here Downeast, the wind jawing back and forth, running east with gales and gouts of rain then swinging west and coating us with heavy, wet snow breaking limbs and uprooting older trees. Power was out all over and the prediction was it'd be a week before the more rural areas were restored. For me that only meant a huge propane bill as my house and my nursery room run on a standby generator soon as the power flicks off.

The afternoon that weather fled into the Gulf of Maine, we were hunkered down in front of the woodstove listening to some vintage Otis Redding, to whom I'd recently introduced Jaime. She was sketching plans for the spa's main yoga room when she glanced up from her pad and said, "Johnny, will the pipes at the farm freeze?"

"Is the water on?" I said.

"Shouldn't it be?" she said.

I didn't want to risk sounding like I was scolding her, so I said. "You've been heating it all winter?"

"Yes," she said, "and I pay Timmy Hankins to plow the driveway so the oil truck can get in."

"Anyone been inside recently?"

Jaime pursed her lips and said, "In late November or early December I set the thermostat on fifty."

Since the worst of the storm was over and the roads would be passable I said, "We should check on the place."

"Now?" Jaime said.

"Might as well," I said, "it'll be dark before we know it."

Jamie insisted we'd need a thermos of fresh coffee, so while she brewed that up, I loaded up my truck with a portable generator, chainsaw, bar oil and fuel, chaps, earphones, and gloves, a peavey, some rope, a heavy duty extension cord and a five gallon can of gas, in order to be prepared for the worst.

It wasn't that I hadn't thought to ask Jaime if the farmhouse had been mothballed, but I try not to give her advice or pry into her favorite projects. I have promised to do whatever site work she needs and help her secure the permits but have offered no suggestions on anything else. I realize there's no chance Jaime and I are a happy-ever-after-December-May-beat-all-the-odds-couple, because no matter how much energy I have someday I won't be able to keep up. I just want our time together to benefit us both with no ugly regrets just a time's up buzzer that tells us it's the moment for her to find someone her own age.

I pulled the truck up to the back door and Jamie hustled out wearing her backpack, carrying a thermos in one hand and a small paper sack in the other. As she swung up into the cab she held out the sack and said, "Can you hold these muffins until I buckle in?"

"Sure," I said. "What's in the pack?"

"My sketch book, some pencils, my phone and a measuring tape," she said.

I didn't need to ask why she'd brought any of those things, because while I was fixed on what might be wrong, I knew she viewed our trip as an adventure.

The driveway was freshly plowed and there was no apparent exterior damage save for a few downed birch limbs well away from the house and barn. I used the grain shovel I keep in the truck to clear the front steps, uncovering an inch of grainy ice on the bricks. Jaime unlocked the front door and I stepped inside for the first time.

The Ragged Head Daigles pursued two endeavors, hay farming or fishing. Jamie's uncle Ronnie was from the agricultural branch of the family and was known to harvest more than hay as a way to make a living. Though he wasn't a big man like Jamie's dad, he, too, died from a massive heart attack while mowing his far field. When he'd not returned home for supper, his girlfriend, Glenna, took their four-wheeler out to look for him and found him slumped over the wheel, the tractor having stalled out on a small rise. When Jamie learned Ronnie willed her the farm, she'd told Glenna she could live there as long as she wanted, but Glenna, who'd only been with Ronnie for a year, headed back to Rhode Island to be near her family.

I'd barely shut the front door and tried the lights—they were on—when Jamie began to sketch in her book and explain her plans for every inch of the house and the barn. Like I said she's an optimist, and her plans were beyond ambitious. The first floor would have an office, kitchen, small café, yoga room, spin machines, showers and whirlpools, massage tables and a steam room and sauna. "Later I'll add outside hot tubs, exercise areas, and maybe like a squash or racquetball court in the barn," she said as she took my hand and tugged me toward the stairs to the second floor, "and wait 'til you see what I'm going to do up here."

Jamie announced that he plan for the second floor was to have an apartment, "Where my two partners will live while we build the business and finish the work in the barn. Then they can have a place out there and this will become a room for overnight or long term guests. Cool eh?"

"I'm impressed," I said, "but that's one hell of a lot of work, and you'll need to get all kinds of permits. But your biggest issue will be your septic. You start adding showers and guest rooms and extra baths you're looking at big bucks. Septic alone might be fifteen grand."

"What if I put in composting toilets?" she asked.

"Think that will go over with your intended clientele?"

"If we make it sound sexy it will," she said.

"How can you make composting toilets sexy?"

"You don't. You make the whole experience sexy by making it environmentally hip."

"What you need is for someone who knows his stuff to look at your plans," I said. "I know site work, and I can do that for you, but materials can get out of hand quickly. And commercial kitchen equipment doesn't come cheap either. Best get some advice."

Jamie headed back downstairs, and I wondered if I'd said something that nettled her because she didn't say a word, just spun on her heels and jogged down the steps. When I caught up with her she said, "Know anyone who can help?"

"I know an architect in Bangor. She's semi-retired, but I know at the very least that she'd take a ride out to see the place. Her name is Pamela Duchenne. She went to school with my mother. She's in her mid-seventies, but still wicked sharp."

"Will you call her?" Jamie said.

"Sure," I said, "soon as the weather clears."

Three weeks later, the farm was free of snow save for where it had drifted in the windrows, and Pamela drove out and spent the entire morning looking at Jamie's dream project. She toured the house from basement to attic, inspected the barn, then perused Jamie's sketches. I was dispatched at eleven-thirty to get some lunch and when I returned Jamie and Pam were coming down from the hill where Glenna had found Ronnie dead on the tractor.

I took the food to the kitchen and watched through the window as the two women sauntered down the brown hillside. They'd pause and one of them would point in one direction then the other. I saw Pamela's head snap back as if she was laughing, a pang of sadness shooting through me, as I recalled how she reminded me of my mom.

Pamela entered the kitchen and announced, "We have a plan."

"And it's ever so cool," Jamie said.

I laid out the food on the table and sat down to listen. "Let me in on the details as we eat," I said.

Pamela opened her sandwich and twisted off the cap on a bottle of water, and said, "Let me start with the upside. She took a bite, chewed it slowly, and said, "Jamie's plans are lofty, but doable. The buildings are both solid and I wouldn't expect she'd encounter any unforeseen issue that would scuttle her plans."

"That's fine, but what is the downside?" I asked.

"Money," Pamela said, "she is way undercapitalized and can't afford to do this at the moment."

"But tell him about the plan," Jamie said.

Pamela stared me straight in the eye and said, "I've known you since the day you came squalling into this world, so I wouldn't bullshit you. I've been in Bangor for almost fifty years. Raised three kids, buried two husbands, and been aching to be back in Ragged Head. Only reason I haven't moved back is I was afraid I'd have nothing to do. I'd miss the library, the theatre, the few friends I have left there, but lately none of that's important."

I must have looked confused because Pamela reached over, tapped my wrist and said, "Be patient." She ate another bite of her sandwich, drank some water and continued," Jamie needs at least another $75,000 cash to get this project rolling. No bank is going to give it to her, so she needs to raise it another way. I looked up the deed before I came out. She's got 52 acres here. I'm willing to buy the six or so that include the top and back side of the hill. If I do that, and you help me put a decent road in, I'll pay Jamie $35,000 for the land, lend her the rest, and do the plans for free. In return I'll be a silent partner at a to be determined percentage.

Jamie was beaming. "Isn't she the best?" she said leaning in to hug me.

I glanced at Pamela. "No well or septic concerns?" I said, "or other permit issues like ADA compliance?"

"I know this area well. She'll get a good perc test and the well's artesian, according to the deed," Pamela said. "The rest should be no problem. She paused, sat forward and said, "When Ronnie died I asked around about the availability of the place, because I've wanted a water view without shoreline taxes. And there's another benefit to me.

My kids live in Oregon, California, and New Mexico. Having hale neighbors and a place to soothe my old bones in my dotage would be a great comfort. And, having a place here might convince the kids to visit."

"There would always be someone here," Jamie said.

"Of course this all works only if you're on board, Johnny," Pamela said, which no one else had called me in years.

"Sure," I said, "let me figure some costs for the road and get some numbers in case she needs a new septic field."

On a cool day in early June, *Land of OM Spa and Yoga LLC* came into being at five-thirty in Monica Mays's office. It took half an hour and then we all went out to Ragged Head Brewing. Pamela and Jamie took turns sketching designs and ideas and Monica and I chatted about her equine rescue farm while we sipped their new Summer Pilsner. Monica left first, then Pamela. Jamie and I stayed for dinner. I didn't want to be alone at home with her where we could have a more intimate discussion than we could in a place where one of us either knew or was related to half the crowd, because for the first time since we've been together I was truly scared of losing her. I know it's inevitable, but I want it to last as long as it can. She's not using me. She believes we'll be the exception to a rule she can't even begin to fathom because she never sees the dark side. What will happen is this. The Spa will become her life. I'll be the permanence and that will get old. It won't be her fault. It's mine for stepping into this in the first place. On New Year's Eve, I could have downed a few quick glasses of bubby and gone home.

On the ride home, Jamie kept her hand on my thigh, and sang old songs she'd learned from her mother, mostly about shipwrecks and lost sailors.

There was a small package on the porch addressed to Jamie. She studied it a second and said, "Oh cool, we can try this out."

"What is it?" I said.

"Let's go in and I'll show you."

I shut the door behind us, and Jamie grabbed my hand and led me into the bedroom. "Get undressed," she said, "Let's see how this is."

"How what is?" I asked.

"This new Japanese massage oil I ordered from a place in California," she said as she tossed a small tube on the bed and took off her t-shirt and bra.

A moment later we were naked. The bed was covered with soft towels. I was lying on my stomach. Jamie was massaging my back. "How does it feel?" she said.

"So good I hope it never ends," I said.

Jamie kneaded and massaged my muscles for several more minutes then rolled me over and rubbed oil on my chest and thighs. She paused to spread oil along her arms and over her breasts and belly, then straddled me. "Rub mine in," she said, handing me the tube, "and put some on my back."

I'll build the road, dig Pamela's foundation, do whatever other site work needs to be done—mostly evenings and weekend—as my busy season is here. I'll offer Jamie my best advice and when I don't know what's best to do, I'll likely know the person who does. She insists I keep strict books so she can pay me back though I won't take her money even if she makes any and I'm not sold she ever will. You see plenty of yoga pants in Ragged Head, but I can't imagine locals paying for the kind of pampering Jamie is convinced will create enough revenue for her and two friends to live on, even if the summer people and tourists keeps them running seven days a week during the season. Her best hope, I think, is to renovate the farm and barn and flip it to some Boston hedge fund manager with a helicopter, though Pamela wouldn't be onboard if she didn't believe the spa can work.

I understand Jamie's motivation to pay me for my work. My grandfather cosigned a loan for my first excavator. My parents gave me twenty-five grand in startup cash, and I can't begin to imagine what that's worth today. At my father's insistence, I paid off the excavator on an accelerated basis, and I promised to repay my parents with interest. When they died, I still owed them four thousand dollars which haunts me to this day.

Downeast summer is ephemeral. This one will be gone, as my grandmother used to say, "In two shakes of a lamb's tail." No one gets younger. Each time I crest March Hill I'll be a bit more worn down, but I'll have Jamie to make that all right until I don't. When she leaves or it's time for me to let her know we've run our course, perhaps I'll be lucky enough to take up with a sturdy sea widow, something Ragged Head is never without. A kind, resilient woman like the ones who brought me food and condolences when the first love of my life died, a woman who knows death, grief, how to mourn with dignity, because Jamie's leaving will be like death, though I won't be able to say I never saw it coming.

Vectors Known and Unknown

Riley Danvers

It wasn't enough,

The time we spent;
How many years did I breathe next to you?
On nights I needed your arms,
Undone by the fracturing of us,
Great barricades kept me away.
Heat does not always
Thaw what's frozen.

You were present but absent,
Oblivious but aware,
Unable to connect or reconnect,

Lost
On trails of your own making.
Viability measured by
Endings coiled into knots,
Desperate breaths.

Maybe that's all we were:
Endings waiting to begin?

Memoir
—after Vijay Seshadri

Darlene Young

The real story of a life is the story of its humiliations,
and mine jolt me from my 5 a.m. drowse
so that my hands fly to my face,
pillow-smashed and bleary,

and only the cat sees,
everyone else in the house dreaming
their own shames at that hour,
my personal God-reckoning hour,
the hour of flinch.

Memoir: once
I denied my guilt
in front of the one I'd betrayed,
both of us knowing I lied.

Once I ignored
the one I loved
to please the one I feared.

I habitually laughed too loud
at my own jokes, and, laughing,
opened my mouth too wide.

Once I said something cold
to someone already hurt.

At 5 a.m., the words I've said
circle like carrion-birds.
I grovel in the sheets like near-roadkill
scraping my way to the bushes
on the far side of the road.

Sailing

Steven Mayer

The wind becomes stronger as I hoist the mainsail up the mast of my small sailing vessel and secure its rigging. I am in the inner Bay of Nelson, heading upwind for Cook Strait between the North and South Islands of New Zealand. By turning my bow into the wind, I can use a zigzag tacking maneuver, routinely changing the set of my sails to progress toward my destination. The spray of saltwater covers my face. My windblown hair is a tangled, curly mess. Adrenaline pulses through my body with a fleeting dose of fear. I am alive in this exhilarating moment. My boat and I move as one.

A day earlier, I sit on my apartment deck, high above the harbor, watching twenty-seven small sailboats cross Cook Strait and disappear on the horizon. I am mesmeric, immersed in mysticism. Larger yachts and sailboats traffic through the harbor. I opt for a nap instead of a stroll around the marina. Sleep impatiently awaits, as I yearn for the morning sun, to become fully alive and sail again.

Later that day, under sail, I move my boat downwind, jibbing with the wind at my back, picking up speed as the late afternoon wind increases, and the sun moves westward. Off my starboard bow is a pod for dolphins begging for a race. I watch them break water as if dancing a ballet, amazed. I let out my jib, a triangular sail at the front of the boat, fixed to the bowsprit, to catch more wind and pick up speed. I am no match for the dolphins. I feel so small, a tiny vessel, on the surface of an immense sea stretching around the world, home to creatures and flora so incredibly beautiful. There is a calm in me like none I have experienced in my lifetime, peace affirming that even in an unfriendly universe, there is a friendly stretch of water on this day on which I can sail my boat safely. I am in love with the sun and sea, the untamed wind, and life on the water.

New Zealand is home to some of the best sailing waters and wind. Their sailors are arguably among the best, as reflected in American Cup performance. It is in their culture and heritage. Harbors moor some of the finest sailing vessels. To be sure, there are powered vessels from small motorboats to larger yachts. Stinkpots, due to their obnoxious noise and smell, are scorned by most who sail. I enjoy walking the docks, admiring the boats, talking to skippers performing maintenance, sharing a beer, hearing their stories, and hoping for an invitation to sail. I love the smell of seafood chowder filling the air, and seagulls flying about in search of a french fry. I am joining a new band of thieves who steal the mysticism of sailing for themselves while others view from their sundecks, unknowingly allowing the theft to occur.

Walking down a dock the next day by the Nelson Yacht Club, I notice a sailing instructor sitting in a tight circle with five young girls around her, likely first graders, playing a game. Each has a short rope less than a meter in length. No game. Serious instruction. The girls are learning to tie nautical knots. When asked to tie a knot, they would do so, and then throw it at another member of the group to check. Laughter erupts. When the locals go sailing, children are often on the boats, performing sailing chores. Most Kiwi youth take a sailing course, on the water, which includes not only navigation but survival. Each captains a small boat, following their instructor in a line, and at command, capsize and rightsize the boat several times until done expediently. At the end of the class, their boats form a tight cluster and sail across the bay out of sight and back. I watch from my deck, binoculars in hand, smiling, as new sailors and mystics are born.

Many don't understand the appeal of sailing. It takes tremendous skill, hard work under harsh conditions (at times), and from afar, seems excruciatingly slow and tedious. Why not opt for a yacht with living quarters twice the size of a sailboat, stocked with twice the wine and beer, and demanding only half the work? Sailing isn't about logic. During my first sailing voyage, I got it! Wind filled the sails as my boat moved swiftly through the water, and I felt nature propel me, invade every fiber of my body, lift me into a new sense of being. My breathing slows to the rhythm of the tide. My spirit unites with the wind filling my sails. It glides me as I maneuver to navigate, change course, adjust my sails, and tighten down my rigging. Once my course is set, I sit back and relax, wind sweeping the sweat from my neck, sun drying it quickly, fully alive, and alone in this exquisite moment.

Metaphors dance around me when I sail straight into a strong wind, confidently. Life may have a strong headwind, resisting my forward motion. Not always, of course, only when I seek to affirm what truly matters. There are periods of calm with no wind—patience and perseverance. There are times of storms with an unforgiving, angry sea—courage and good judgment. There are spaces of rest, to anchor and swim in clear aqua-blue waters of some remote cove—rest and recovery. There are nights without land in sight, with penetrating stillness inside, with the universe close above—reverence and faith in life. All welcome the mystic to be at home here, in their embrace, to navigate by the stars and charts, beheld by the wind in the sails and our soul, this unseen force of nature that moves us in our journey of life.

Sailing

When I have trouble sleeping, I dream of sailing far away, to a place I have never been, one that I will never leave, a different home and beginning, a new lifetime, somewhere among the stars, an infinite sea, somewhere close to whom I love, sailing on.

The Question

Peter Vertacnik

Midway through
Our back-and-
Forth about where to eat,
You pause, taking
A breath like a crisp page
Turning.
        "What if,"
You say, "someday,
I needed something
From you, to live? A kidney,
Maybe? Would you?"

"Oh, we'd never be
A match," I say.
"I mean, you know, sometimes
Not even family, like, not
Blood relatives even, and we—"

"No, I know," you say.
"It wouldn't work. It's not
Likely ever to happen anyway.
But what if? That's all.

Could you just say it
For me?"
    Along my sleeve
Your index finger traces a crease
While we wait.

'I Do' to Inamoratas' Tattoos

Nicole Cortino

Reach with your dominant hand
with your silky wrist that reads in cursive
"Keep me wild."

I do,
in young daydreams of a one-bedroom apartment
in Colorado centered between a fashion design school
and a children's welfare hospital,

in confrontational conversations, under a red plastic roof,
fingertips meet damp cheeks and chapped lips
surrounded by wooden play chips,

in the run from punishment of no more nuzzled necks
or painted pages, no more fountain fireworks after chess
on a picnic table where the breeze smells of a fresh future,
I do.

For you,
who gifted a beaded reminder to breathe, I, too, reach
with the opposite hand to hold and slender wrist
with the same font that reads, "Keep me safe."

I will,
my *forever and always and always and AND always and love,*
wildly do the same.

Shoehorned

Linda Drach

Among the last things you touched
was your long-handled shoehorn
made of rigid plastic, curved,
navy blue, a practical tool to help you
stay independent. You'd tired
of me, kneeling before you, coaxing
your heels into sturdy slip-on loafers,
adjusting your socks, while you looked away.

Your other shoes were gone: the steel-toed
work boots, the oxblood leather Oxfords, the high-top
sneakers with their ladders of laces, the flip-flops,
the hip boots, even the slippers
with their fuzzy sheepskin linings, your half
of the matching pairs we got that year
for Christmas, all of that, let go—replaced

by the shoehorn, which I find on the bed,
lying by my pillow, left there after
you slipped on your shoes, then

picked up the gun, carefully placed
your wallet on the dresser, emptied
your pockets, emptied out

the pocket watch, the pearl-
handled penknife, carefully,
the change. You are gone.

I Imagine Watching My Father's Autopsy

Cecil Morris

At the autopsy the doctor prizes
open the secret cabinet, sternum
split and spread, and lifts the small red fortress,
the heart, now pale and fallen still and quiet,
like the morning after thunder storm
without the clean smell, the breath caught and held
and waiting for sound that does not come.
Then the metal click of small tools put down,
of the scale pan moving, weight calculated,
the heft of his one life measured and noted
in matter-of-fact, talking-to-oneself voice.
In the muscle's four small chambers, he finds
an antique card catalog, the blond oak,
the long wooden drawers, stiff manila
cards, hand-typed—the popular ones thumb-smudged
and worn, their corners gone soft: the slow rise
and roll of a big ship in open sea,
Jimmie's blue voice yodeling, tobacco
horn worms long as his finger, hanging leaves
to dry, the wet slap of waves, his father's
big hands, Zane Grey, fishing with his two kids,
the river's bright noise, the slick slip of thumb

clearing guts, Shirley and Annie laughing,
Andy, Barn, and Matlock, Mom's fried chicken.
The doctor ignores this spill from his heart
and notes only the occlusions and scars,
his gloved fingers closing the four chambers.

The Dacha

Susanne Davis

Chloe Henderson stood looking out the window of her room at the Herzen Inn. It was 10 p.m., but because of the White Nights, that evening in St. Petersburg, Russia was as bright as noon. She'd been invited to the dacha of Katerina Olgenov, a prestigious editor, and when Katerina stepped out of her car at the curb, Chloe rushed downstairs to meet her. They'd met at a cocktail party the previous year and their friendship had deepened through a year's worth of emails, resulting in the invitation. Katerina greeted Chloe with a hug and swung her suitcase into the trunk, teasing that it took up more room than the gardening tools and the weekend's food, combined. She told Chloe 2.5 million people—half the city's population left each weekend for their dachas.

"Did you bring me bulbs from your estate?" she asked.

Chloe shook her head. "I don't own an estate, Katerina. It's just a house. I'm sorry about the bulbs, though. I read that any live plant was prohibited because of the possibility of carrying contamination."

"Oh, but I wanted a few," Katerina pouted. "You wrote about your gardens so beautifully. To have a few plants would remind me of you. Did you know dacha means something given?"

"No, I didn't," Chloe said. "I'm sorry; I was afraid of trouble."

Katerina waved her hand. "What could they do? Well, never mind, we will have fun together in the garden."

Gardening and love of the land had been a topic in their emails over the winter. Chloe tried to imagine a culture still so tied to the land, migrating back to it every weekend. They drove toward Karelia, two to three hours north of St. Petersburg depending on the traffic and just 120 kilometers from Finland. Along the way they stopped at a Russian version of Sam's Club and jostled through aisles with all the other commuters, selecting coffee, breakfast pastry, marinated chicken kabobs, and cherry pie. They got back into the car with their bags, moving north again, with the spires of the pines pricking the night sky and conversation turning personal.

Chloe asked after Katerina's children.

Katerina had referred to her handicapped son the previous summer, but now she expanded the story. At age eight, Sergei's spine curved and doctors diagnosed scoliosis. By age ten he couldn't stand straight; he had to peer out from under his arm to see the world.

"My first husband and I took Sergei to doctors in Siberia, the best doctors in Russia and those doctors told us to prepare for him to die."

In Russia, Sergei would have died, she explained, but she couldn't accept that. So she brought him to the United States, to Boston, where doctors turned them away saying it was too late, then to Johns Hopkins where doctors agreed to operate for a half million dollars.

"I worked a second job, for a rich man in Luxemburg who paid for the surgery."

"What did you do for him?" Chloe asked.

"I do whatever he wants," Katerina replied. "I'm still paying it off." She was driving 90 mph on the narrow road, telling the story as smoothly as she shifted the car. "Tell me, what do you think of globalism?" she asked.

Chloe stammered something about regretting the export of American fast food.

"Globalism is inevitable." Katerina turned down a narrow dirt road cutting through the forest.

"We're here," she announced when the headlights hit a cluster of buildings.

"What a cute shed," Chloe said.

"The outhouse," Katerina smiled. "Do not be too critical. Our dacha is not your estate."

Figures moved toward them in the dark. A tall man wearing a blazer and hair pulled into a ponytail kissed Katerina.

"This is my husband, Yegeni."

Chloe knew Yegeni was a well-known poet in Russia.

He folded himself into a Buddhist bow to greet her, then took her suitcase from the trunk and climbed the dacha steps.

Inside, they gathered around the table of a screened porch, and Katerina introduced Chloe to some other guests, a 34-year-old Russian writer, Alexsandar, and his charge, 17-year-old Pasha. Katerina hadn't mentioned other guests to her. Chloe felt as though she was entering a Russian novel.

"Sergei is asleep," Yegeni said to Katerina's questioning gaze.

"You will meet him tomorrow then," Katerina told Chloe. "Let us have some pie."

They sat down at the table with a bottle of wine and the cherry pie.

Alexsandar started talking about the greatness of "Mother Russia," and the problems the fledgling democracy had encountered after he claimed America had abandoned her. "Once the communist government fell, America was no longer interested in helping us. Many more people struggle now than did under communism."

"Are you saying you would rather go back to Soviet rule?" Katerina asked sharply.

Alexsander pressed his back against the chair. "Many people would. What did Americans feel about NATO bombing Serbia?" he asked Chloe.

Chloe couldn't remember when Serbia had been bombed and she knew better then to tell him Americans hardly spoke of the Kosovo War. "I 'm not sure," she said.

"NATO bombed without UN approval, they claimed against military targets, but over 2000 civilians were killed and over 200,000 Serbs forced out of Kosovo." Alexsander spoke as if the bombings had been recent. But they weren't. Chloe thought about the other side of the story, ethnic cleansing of Albanians by the Serbians in Kosovo.

"Alexsander, we have to let go," Katerina said.

"—Do you know CS Lewis?" Alexsander asked Chloe.

"CS Lewis?" She'd read him of course, but no, she couldn't quote him.

Alexsander ran his hand through his hair, making it stand on end. "Give me all of you!" he slid to the edge of his chair, toward her. Sweat slicked his forehead. He paused to be sure that Pasha was paying attention.

When Pasha nodded, he continued.

"I don't want to only prune a branch here and a branch there; rather I want the whole tree out! Hand it over to me, the whole outfit, all of your desires, all of your wants and wishes and dreams. Turn them ALL over to me, give yourself to me and I will make of you a new self—in my image."

Alexsander thumped his hand over his heart. "My will shall become your will. My heart shall become your heart." He slid back, satisfied. "Do you know where that is from?"

Chloe shook her head.

"*Mere Christianity*," Pasha answered.

"Very good, Pasha." Alexsander smiled without taking his eyes off Chloe. "When you see suffering, it is here," he tapped his heart. "I want to caution you: A person should not be too calm with another person's pain."

He and Yegeni were drinking vodka now. They offered it to Chloe, but she declined. She couldn't quote a single selection of English literature and certainly, no Russian. If she got drunk she wouldn't be able to carry on any conversation at all. She wasn't sure what CS Lewis had to do with the bombing of Serbia. She felt completely out of her comfort zone. Alexsandar asked what Russians she'd read and she named them: Dostoevsky, Tolstoy, Nabokov, Gogol, Pushkin, Chekhov, and when she said Akhmatova, he and Yegeni agreed that Marina Tsvetaeva, Akhmatova's contemporary who fled Russia, returned, then committed suicide, was the better poet.

Alexsandar asked which university she taught at as if he doubted her intellectual ability. She ignored what she perceived as a slight and asked where he was from in Russia.

Alexsander replied, "I am from the Caucasus region where the people are very strong, made of iron. Only iron. They do not like the influence of outsiders."

"You are Russian, Alexsandar," Katerina said. "And our democracy has given you opportunities to travel and write and speak, has it not?" Before he could protest, she pushed her chair back from the table and nodded for Chloe to follow.

Katerina climbed a narrow flight of stairs and led Chloe down the hall to an alcove under the eaves and gestured to a mattress on the floor. The clock read 1 a.m. Chloe thanked Katerina and curled up into a ball to stare out the window at the full communion wafer of a moon. The evening had overloaded her senses. Whatever Russian novel she may have entered, she was seeing she didn't understand even the basic plot.

Chloe woke to the smell of jasmine and coffee. Downstairs she found herself alone in the room she'd been too tired to take in the night before. Jasmine grew up the wall and the sun shone through the lace curtains, spilling into a tin sink. On the far wall, a wooden cupboard held plates and mugs. In the center of the room the four straight-backed chairs had been pushed in around the table, where someone had set a bowl of steaming pasta.

Chloe plugged in an electric water pot. While waiting for it to heat, she poked her head into the master bedroom. Colorful quilts and blankets covered a king-sized bed; the room looked like a happy playground for two. She backed out, mixed water and instant coffee and went outside to find Katerina. A canvas of color surrounded her: lilacs, irises, phlox, columbine, bleeding hearts, daisies, poppies, and azaleas. Chloe had never seen so much variety.

"Did you sleep well?" Katerina asked.

"Yes, very well." Chloe said.

"I would like to introduce you to Sergei," Katerina said as she stepped aside.

The first thing Chloe noticed was the long pointed nose protruding from Sergei's face. Below the nose, his mouth revealed his teeth, some angled, others straight. He wore a baseball cap that cast a shadow, but his luminous eyes couldn't be hidden. Chloe had never seen such light. His black nylon zip-up hid his frame. He came closer and peeked at Chloe from under the brim of his hat, head cocked like a bird, watching her.

"It is nice to meet you, Sergei." Chloe willed her gaze to stay locked with his so she wouldn't stare at his body.

He smiled and then floated away, leaving she and Katerina to plant and tend flowers. They both seemed a bit shy with each other in the bright morning. Aside from Katerina giving directions, they didn't speak much as they worked. Voices floated toward them from a nearby tree, where Alexsander tutored Pasha in his studies. Chloe felt Alexsander's eyes on her and was relieved when Yegeni came and suggested she and Katerina join him for a bike ride.

They cycled along a stony path out of the little dacha village, with Katerina and Yegeni expertly dodging deep potholes and jutting rocks as they chatted back and forth. Just moving forward required Chloe's constant vigilance, she didn't try to join the conversation. Yegeni, seeing her struggle, circled back.

"You must change speeds to go faster," he offered.

"Thanks, but I don't want to go faster," she said.

"Tsst," he shook his head reproachfully and seemed to lose interest in a person who wouldn't try harder. He peddled back to Katerina. They rode along the path for another mile or so until they came upon a high bluff. Peering over the edge, they showed her a river filled with rapids and strong currents.

"There are two lakes," Yegeni said. "An upper and a lower. This river connects them."

"The new Russians," Katerina pointed to the jet skis below. "They have much money, but no skill. They are not professionals."

"No. Not professionals," Yegeni agreed, pointing out the smaller number of kayaks bobbing along like persistent dreams, their bright colors refusing to be dashed, while on jet skis the new Russians chopped the water loudly.

The three of them mounted their bikes again and rode on to a small store—one that sold drinks and snacks and sold camping and bike gear. They ordered lemon lime soda and sat at a picnic table on the patio.

A man at a table near them glared in their direction, at Chloe. H shook his head and swore loudly in Russian. Chloe didn't know what he was saying, but she could see the woman and child with him looked uncomfortable, as did others sitting on the patio. Yegeni and Katerina exchanged glances.

"We should move on," Yegeni said, ushering them away from the patio, back to the bikes.

Before Chloe could ask any questions, Yegeni looked at his watch and spoke in Russian to Katerina.

"Yegeni must meet his friends." Katerina shook her head as if to say what can one do. Yegeni laughed like a boy being scolded.

"This friend is very pretty, but Yegeni tells me I am jealous. Tell me I have no reason," she said to him.

"No, you do not." Yegeni smiled and kissed her cheek before getting on his bike and peddling off in a new direction.

Chloe could feel Katerina's thoughts follow him.

They rode, the two of them, to the shore of the upper lake where Katerina stripped off her clothes. She was wearing a bikini. She seemed surprised Chloe didn't have a bathing suit under her clothes. "You could skinny dip," she said. "No one will see you."

But Chloe insisted she was happy to sit on a rock and wait. She watched as Katerina plunged right into the cold water, diving again and again, going further out each time. Chloe could almost feel her turmoil dissipating into the choppy water. When she came back to shore she seemed calmer. She dressed and without a word, mounted her bike and signaled for Chloe to follow her back to the dacha.

When much later Yegeni returned, Katerina looked up from where they'd gone back to work in the garden and gave him a searching look.

Yegeni looked away.

"May I take a picture of you two?" Chloe asked, trying to fill the awkward silence. "To bring home?"

Katerina frowned at her husband. "I'm not feeling romantic. How shall we pose?"

But Yegeni didn't seem discouraged. "A picture is a good idea." He whispered something in Katerina's ear and her resistance melted as she leaned toward him.

"Demeter! Yes, I love it. And you are Zeus."

So, Yegeni took up his pose. Starting at the edge of the garden he came crouching toward his wife, the goddess of nature. Pasha had given Katerina a bow and arrow and she aimed the arrow straight at Yegeni.

Chloe held her breath, waiting.

Yegeni paused for just a millisecond, scanning Katerina's face, and then satisfied, he slinked closer, grabbed her around the waist, and kissed her neck.

Katerina squealed, delighted, and fell into his embrace.

Chloe, so drawn into the moment, forgot to take the picture. And no one else seemed to notice. They declared they were hungry and set about preparing dinner.

That night, as they ate shaslik by the fire, and Pasha told a story.

"I am the elder son of Alexander Gomav. My sister Masha is older, 19. My brother Misha, my sister Legera and two others, Petre is the son of my stepmother and my father. Alegra is the daughter of my mother and another man. My father was an engineer in Soviet times.

With the collapse of the Soviet regime, he lost his job. Now, he delivers to orchards fruit and vegetable seeds from a botanics company. We grow many fruits and vegetables. Last year, my brothers, sister Masha, our babushka, and I, fixed our roof. Our house has a kitchen, dining room, and three other rooms."

"And your mother, Pasha?" Chloe asked. With two young sons at home she couldn't imagine being left out of their stories.

"We are in communication, but because of the distance we do not see her often. I did not see her much when I was growing up."

Chloe had no business to probe his pain and she felt the others silently judging her for doing so.

"My mother has an interesting life," Pasha said as if to end the subject, and then, more sternly, "I hope I can become the kind of man who deserves my father."

Alexsander frowned at Chloe. "Let's practice with the bow and arrow."

"No, let us play a different game," Katerina suggested. "Enough vodka for you, Sergei."

Sergei took another sip from the bottle he'd been trying to hide in his lap.

Yegeni jumped up, hung a target on the side of the shed, and assembled the bow and arrow. "Our guest first."

Chloe felt Alexsandar's eyes on her. She felt he was not only expecting her to fail, but also willing her to. She took a deep breath, drew back the arrow and sent it into the target, where it quivered: not a bull's eye, but very close. Yegeni nodded, but Alexsander shrugged and instead of taking a turn at the target, went to join Pasha and Sergei drinking by the fire. Chloe put down the bow and looked for Katerina. Yegeni pointed to the dacha.

When Katerina did not answer her call, Chloe climbed the stairs to her mattress in the little alcove. At some point she fell asleep.

She woke to loud voices, doors slamming and a car motor starting. It roared off into the night and Chloe huddled, straining to hear more, but no other sounds came and eventually she fell back asleep.

The next morning she found Katerina in her garden deadheading flowers with a giant pair of sheers, snipping away until colorful blooms swung free from the weight of their shriveled compatriots. She wore a cotton peasant skirt with ruffles sweeping the ground as she swung the shears.

Chloe settled on the stonewall beside her. "What did I hear last night?"

"Sergei," Katerina said, answer and exasperation in the one word. "He got very drunk by the fire and rode his bicycle into the forest."

Chloe laughed; the image of anyone riding drunk through the forest seemed funny until she saw the anger cross Katerina's face.

"He could have hurt himself," Katerina admonished. "His bones are very brittle. If he were to fall he would not heal as others heal."

Sergei appeared from the dacha then and hovered at the garden's edge. Chloe imagined him with splintered bones floating beneath the surface of his skin. She didn't know what to say. The thought was so terrible.

She watched Sergei as he slipped his camera out of its case. Chloe thought he was going to take a picture of his mother until she saw something flitting in front of his lens. Sergei smiled at her and very slowly stepped toward her and sat down beside her. He put out a hand and the flitting object came and hovered over his open palm. A hummingbird, its little wings a blur of motion waiting while he snapped a picture.

Katerina shook her head at him and went back to work. Her green eyes flashed. Her cropped hair shone a burnished red and her tube top squeezed her breasts together, leaving her chest and slender collarbones exposed to the morning air. Behind her the morning sky turned lavender and then the pale gray of any morning, but in that moment before it turned, Chloe saw Katerina between two worlds.

The light changed, and the moment ended, but when Yegeni came out of the house, holding a coffee mug, Chloe knew he was going to break Katerina's heart and she couldn't make herself give him a greeting.

"Where is Alexsander?" Katerina asked, crossly.

Yegeni shrugged. "He left."

"But Pasha is still here?"

"I will bring Pasha back to St. Petersburg in a couple of days."

"Where did Alexsander go?" Katerina pressed on. "I promised his mother...I would watch out for him."

"He felt you were mad about Sergei's drinking." Yegeni said.

"I heard his phone ring in the night," Katerina said. "Who was calling him?"

"I don't know." Yegeni backed away, got on his bike and rode into the forest. If he knew more, he was not going to tell. Chloe was happy to see him go.

Chloe went into the house and boiled water to clean the dishes. It felt good, cleaning, but it didn't help Katerina in any real way and it didn't explain the contradictions of the weekend.

Yegeni returned just as they were getting in the car to go back to the city. He bowed to Chloe as she got in. Chloe nodded, stiffly.

Katerina wasn't happy that he was staying at the dacha, but she didn't say so to Chloe. The ride back to St. Petersburg was quiet, with Sergei sleeping in the back seat.

When they neared the city, Chloe decided to try to reach her friend. "Are you alright, Katerina?" she asked.

She hoped Katerina might open up about her relationship, but instead she said, "I am worried about Alexsander. His mother is a dear friend. She shared with me her worry that lately his ideas get extreme and he has swung to a far position."

"Why was he quoting CS Lewis and what was he saying about his homeland?"

"There has been a clash of religions in that region for 2000 years," Katerina said. "He has become ultra religious and political. I hope he did not make you too uncomfortable." She pulled her hair back from her eyes and smiled. "I do not think you will forget us." They had reached the Herzen Inn at a busy time of day and staying parked at the curb wasn't possible.

Sergei got out of the car to give Chloe a hug and she hugged him back carefully, thinking of his bones floating beneath his skin. He climbed into the front passenger seat, waiting for his mother.

Katerina placed Chloe's luggage on the sidewalk and embraced her. "I envy you," she said. "You are free. I am not free." She slammed the trunk closed and got behind the wheel and drove away, ending the weekend much as it started, with Chloe at a loss for proper words.

The two women did not speak again before Chloe got on the plane back to the United States. A day after her return, there was news coverage of a deadly terror attack in Russia. The news commentator likened the brutality to attacks of the terrorist Shamil Basleyev. Chloe googled and read about this militant who'd been killed years earlier. He was from the region Caucasus, Alexsandar's homeland and had been a leader of the Chechen movement. Chloe read more--that the Caucasus Mountains, Alexsander's homeland, spanned several countries and that the region was cut by deep gorges, a wild and untamed place. Islam and Christianity had ancient roots there. Articles described the Caucasus Mountains in biblical terms quoting the Old Testament and foretelling precipitous events arising from the region. The picture became clearer now, Alexsander's love for the CS Lewis quote, his statement that the people of the Caucasus region were made only of iron, his resistant to outside influence, and Katerina's worry about his extreme views.

Chloe thought how the old Russian stories of Tolstoy and Chekhov were not what she had encountered at the dacha and she couldn't yet say what the new stories were.

A few weeks later an email arrived from Katerina. It said only "I thought you might like this photo that Sergei took that day at the dacha."

Chloe downloaded the attachment—a photo of the hummingbird with Sergei's hand stretched out beneath it. The miniature wings green in a blur of motion.

When Chloe went to her garden, she went immediately her prize dahlias, an heirloom variety given by her grandmother. There weren't many and she wanted her gift to be generous so she dug all but one bulb, packaged them in a box under many layers of wrap and drove to the post office. She asked for the box to be delivered airmail without even asking how much that would cost. She hoped Katerina might receive the bulbs before her next trip to the dacha.

The postal worker asked her—did the package contain anything prohibited or perishable? And Chloe shook her head no—for, she thought, how could the healing language of peace be prohibited?

Artist

Steven Mayer

I watched her closely my little
girl, only six years old, coloring
in her coloring books at first
between the lines
later ignoring them
limited by crayons, form
her creativity bounded.

Showing her how to trace
images carefully, even
changing the lines, shapes
drawing freely, discarding
crayons and coloring books,
discovering watercolor paints
brushes, canvas, and more.

I watched closely, her
mood changed
imagination took flight
joyful expression; artful play
seriously focused on detail,

discarding what she didn't like
displaying what she did.

She grew, her art grew
blooming into a life passion
pen and ink sketches
color delicately added
vibrant and compelling
like the person she became
my little girl.

Risk Assessment

Devon Balwit

The chickens are old enough
to sleep outside, but my son won't

allow it. Each night, he returns them
to his closet, where they huddle

beneath a hot bulb and complain
about the unwanted narrowing

of their horizons. My boy dreads
his favorite, the smallest, falling

to a raccoon. Just another night,
he says, nightly. I understand—

wanting to delay, forever,
his driving, fearful of an icy road,

a blinding rain, a drunk. I imagine
him in my closet, knees

drawn to his chin, cramped
and irritable, but safe. Safe.

CHRONOSCOPE 250: How Do I?

John Walser

When the levee leaks
when the water rises
when the mud disappears
and bushes
and cars

when the highways turn
to waterways:
the waterways to broadening:
the broadening to vastness:
the vastness moves
to washing away

thunder, lightning

how do I convince
a two year old
(our tiny love!)
who wants
to go outside
to touch the trees
the way the two

of us have
each season
maple, birch, elm
to watch
the leaf shift canopy
to make the dying
tongues of irises
spring back and forth:
to hold woodchips
like tickets
that came in

how do I convince her
how do I convince myself
to stay inside?

The Silver Streaker

Bernard W. Duffy

We were on the third lap inside the Washington Square Mall. It was only a few minutes before opening and Phil and Connie, this morning's pacesetters for our walking group, The Silver Streakers, had gone turbo. Yeah, well, they didn't have a knee replaced six months ago. Or lose their spouse of 37 years two months ago. And not heard back from their daughter or grandkids for three maybe four weeks now. As those show-offs pulled away, I remember trying to say:

I (pant) can't (pant) can't (pant) really keep up. Can't.

I sat on the bench by the Welcome Center—breathing hard—and watched my herd of fat-asses double-time past the escalators. Howie was passing Warren on the outside of the turn. That's just plain disrespectful.

My new knee was angry with me and really letting me know it.

I hope Roxie got the money for her Nutcracker costume in time. Last year a mouse, this year a snowflake. I'll fly down to see it right before Christmas. First one without Elizab—

Lord Almighty! Christ, that hurts!

That's what I get for taking a week off. But I had a cold. Nobody enjoys exerting themselves with a runny nose. Now I can smell the bakery. I hate this diet. Elizabeth would have kept me on this diet no matter what. If I have to buy more pants... What's after XXL? Is there really another X? So embarrassing.

Two brightly illuminated young hikers beamed down on me from a mountain, their teeth whiter than the snow surrounding their ridiculously fit forms. *Made in Oregon!* shouted the adver-tising copy. Metal gates clattered open, announcing another day of retail and all the hopes and dreams that go with it. Mall security turned some keys and a few weekday shoppers trickled in.

I checked my phone. Still no response from my daughter. Maybe I came on a little strong with advice regarding Roxie's ear infection. But, Jeez, Pam—come on—at least let me know you got the funds. And how was I supposed to plan a visit without a firm date? Sure, it wasn't for a couple of months, but what if the airfares go up? So, I checked the airlines. Then email. Then the weather. Rain possible tonight between one and five. Not even a quarter of an inch. I'll close the windows anyway, before going to bed. God, my knee was hurting.

Peetah-doop! A message. Pam? No. Shari's was offering that pie deal for seniors again. Maybe shoot over there before I go to—

Darn it. Phil and Connie turned the distant corner, chugging hard. I got up and headed for the restroom—always a good excuse—behind the Welcome Center. Darn it again: the custodian had blocked it off for cleaning. I abruptly changed course and headed for the nearby escalator to use the restroom up off the Food Court. What ever would we do without escalators? If I had to ac-tually climb these stairs I'd starve.

Coming out of the men's room, I wanted coffee but not a single food outlet had opened. I wasn't about to stand in line at the Starbucks on the main floor. Maybe try that new drive-thru. If I ran into any of the group on my way out, I'd tell them that:

I had a doctor's appointment.

That Shari's was doing that pie thing.

That it was going to rain tonight.

And that my daughter had gotten back to me with the dates for my trip.

I was getting all this in order as I rode down the escalator... when I saw the strangest thing.

On the up escalator, ten yards away, was a small child, a girl, as it turned out. She could on-ly be seen by the little pink pig ears on the top of her hat, and the tiny hand that gripped the escala-tor's black rubber rail. This little upright piglet seemed to be riding to the unopened Food Court without any adult accompaniment. I swung my gaze a full one-eighty, looking down to the mall floor, then up to the Food Court. No, there was absolutely no parent attending to her. The escalator was entirely empty of guardians. This child is totally lost and alone, I thought. As I reached the bottom, and hurriedly moved to the base of the up escalator, I saw the girl, in a matching pink quilted jacket, reach the top of the very long escalator—trip, almost fall—and then disappear.

This wasn't right. I had to see about this.

Ignoring my knee, I bounded up the up escalator, which resulted in double speed and triple pain. Halfway up, already out of breath, I had to stop and just ride. Who knows? Maybe her par-ents had just gotten ahead of her and she was safely back in their care.

Nope. Here she comes, descending the down side to my up side. Man, this kid was on the move! Upon reaching the top, I limp-can-tered—still out of breath— back down the set of stairs that divided the escalators. My knee was literally barking, howling for mercy. When I reached the main floor, she was gone.

This was not my child, but once parental instincts fire, she might as well be. What if she wanders out to the parking lot? What if she rides the escalator again and an untied shoelace catches in the teeth, the grinding maw of those moving metal steps? What if a sick person grabs her for any number of horrific reasons?

My Elizabeth would be so proud of how I'm handling this. She would understand how this noble, selfless pursuit was inflaming my knee. And how to rub the ointment on it.

The mall, open a mere ten minutes, was very quiet, with only a few shoppers in the dis-tance. Another clump of mall-walkers was thundering through. This was a rival walking gang—The Beaverton Breeze—that annoyed the heck out of us because it traveled counter-clockwise. Clockwise is the rule. Maybe the unspoken rule, but still the rule. Which is why we suspended our good manners to sneeringly refer to them as The Pudgy Plodders.

As these determined plush-soled souls waddled by, I asked a pleasant couple, straggling to catch the clump, if they had seen my girl. No? Okay, that meant This Little Piggy had gone to Mar-ket: to the left. I began an urgent trot down the big hall. I was not only out of breath, my knee throbbing, but beginning to pale with fear. That aw-ful dry cotton-mouth was happening and my stomach was painfully filling with acid. Which meant no Key Lime at Shari's. Alternate gener-ous slices of Coconut Cream and Boston Cream oughta do it.

Hey. Focus.

Half-jogging, half-limping, I began frantically zigzagging be-tween mid-aisle pop-up ki-osks. I stopped at every store on both sides of the big hall, bursting into:

Anthropologie: *Have you seen...?*
Game Stop: *Did a little...?*
Sunglass Hut: *All by herself!*
The Duck Store: *Pig...she's a pig!*

The Star Wars Store: *No bigger than Yoda!*

At the end of the hall, I looked left then right. There she was. The tiniest thing, toddling to-wards Target. Must be seventy yards down the corridor. Still entirely alone. She must have, at this point, wandered a good half mile through this enormous shopping center, a three- or four-year-old child, all on her own. Not one adult has at-tempted to save her from the Escalator Mangle-Monster, the Wheels of Death Crusher-Bus, the Claws of the Kid-Grabber-Nappers Gang. Not one other person.

Only I.

I alone have flung my tri-focal eyeglasses to the floor. I alone have ripped open my L.L. Bean shirt to reveal...*the Big Red Double S.*

I fly down the hall, 30 feet in the air, muscular arms extended, shops and vending kiosks whizzing by. In the distance I see the huge glass door of a store swung open by two chattering teens as they exit. The tiny girl enters, completely unseen. Within three seconds I touch down—the red-booted foot of my good leg artistically extended, my silvery cape fluttering above—at the store:

Apple.

I am halted by a phalanx of blue shirted nerd-geeks, swarming me like Lex Luther's min-ions, demanding my appointment time, my model number, my operating system. Beyond them, halfway into the store, I see my pig-child walk up to a young woman who is intently hunched over a new cell phone. The child tugs on her mom's sleeve. The mother looks down, smiles at her baby, softly strokes those soft pig ears. Goes back to her cell.

Geniuses.

I squeeze my eyes shut, initiate Omni-Vision. I see a shadowy figure by the fountain, be-hind a potted palm, his greedy eyes locked on the little girl. I see the pig hat lying outside on the pavement, printed darkly with tire treads. At the top of the escalator I see fresh bright blood flow-ing from the grinning steel jaws.

Upon opening my eyes, I realize: this girl, *my* girl, does not be-long to this woman anymore. I cannot allow it. With my Super-Chill breath I freeze everyone in the store. I pick up the child, cradle her in my arms and fly down the hall, my cape snapping in the wind as I slalom kiosks. Out the front entrance and up, up and away: to my Fortress of Silver Streaker Solitude!

Where my beloved Elizabeth is waiting with open arms to care for yet another rescued child.

Ten years from now, this one will debut triumphantly as:

Pig Girl! Protector of Lost Mall Children.

I will have taught her to fly, to disable escalators with the laser-magnetos in her robotic corkscrew tail, to stop a speeding bus with a single trotter and to render bad guys senseless with her Super-Squeal.

Yes. This. All this.

After a quick stop at Shari's.

38th and Chicago, Mpls., MN

Karen Sandberg

The closer I get
    More store fronts are boarded
The closer I get
    More people walking
I see all ages all colors all hairstyles
    Families, teens, aged
    Small children asking why
    Billy Graham crisis chaplains
    Men with marijuana flags
    Men with feather in long braided hair
    Women in jingle dresses ready to pray
    Elder black men with sad faces
The closer I get
    Conversation quiets
The closer I get
    I hear chanting
    Smell sage
    Hear his name
        George
    Chanting George Floyd

Hear the names of all the black faces
    In the sage in the air
    In the catalog of the murdered
    In the sacred powerful air

The Darkness Leans Close In
(Winter Solstice)

Madronna Holden

I have no desire to ascend
to that lofty place shared
by warriors and priests.

Mine is a simple
dream of violets:
of tiny green
and purple
things.

My heart is a matter of necessity.

I would stand here on this shore
where the sky talks to itself
in sunlight and clouds—

suspended between birth and death
in this perfect flawed world.

I would stretch the way
the earth stretches,
cell by cell—here
for all the root
and stalk of it.

I do not wish to calibrate
the world to my dreams.

I do not wish to walk
in and out of time.

I only wish to slip words
into my pocket as small lighted things
keeping faith in the memory of the sun
on the shortest day
of the year,

home to earth because
the mountains are,

home to sky because of the
silver corner of moon in my eye,
home to the storm because color
has promised itself to rainbows,

thunder has promised itself to sound,

and life has promised itself to hope.

Mom

Marc Jampole

Sometimes she treated us like pelican children,
feeding us blood straight from her veins,
sometimes we were rat babies in a famine
and she gnawed into our bellies
and sucked the fat and muscle off our bones
for sustenance, not of her body,
but of her murdered and murdering soul.

Skin the Cat

Daniel Pié

My dad looked small down there in the water last summer. His voice was smaller, too.

It boomed at first—"Geronimooooo!"—but kept getting quieter until I heard this gigantic splash. It happened so fast. One second, I was staring at the cottage cheese around his stomach. Then, the next second, he ran past me and disappeared over the edge.

He started yelling up at me to jump off the rock, too. He didn't sound like thunder, though, the way he does when he and Mom are fighting. And, anyway, it was hard to hear with the cicadas clicking like crazy and the river making slapping sounds against the boulders.

"C'mon, Dell. Let 'er rip and get down here. The water is really nice."

The sun was shining through the trees and the rays made sparkles on the river all around him. I thought the top of his head was one of them for a second, but then I could see that all that white was just the way the water pushed his little bit of hair to the side.

"What are you doing?" Dad shouted and threw his hands up in the air. I was trying to find a path down to the water. "Just jump."

"It's too high."

"Nonsense. You can do it. I'll grab you when you hit the water. No sweat."

But I *was* sweating, worse than during the long hike up to the ledge. I tried to keep my knees from wobbling, but they kept knocking into each other, and my sweat was changing into goosebumps. I wanted to go back the way we came, even if the gobs of gnats and mosquitos swarmed around us again on the trail.

"I can't do it!"

"Look at me, Dell. Trust me, son."

I wanted to. I really did. But then I saw some rocks that were kinda like steps down to the river. Dad was waiting with this frown on his face. He was big again.

We didn't talk hardly at all as we walked along the riverbank. I tried to put my feet in the tracks that he made, but mostly they were too far apart.

"Where are we going, Dad?"

I could tell he was disappointed. The corner of his mouth sort of crinkled when he looked at me over his shoulder. My face got really hot and my bottom lip got jittery.

"This will eventually get us back to our camp."

"Oh, okay. Good. Dad?"

"What is it, Dell?"

"You're not gonna tell Connie that I didn't jump, are you?"

Dad and Mom think my sister is such an angel. I know that she—my sister, Connie, I mean—is more like a devil, and I'm not saying that just because she got me into this fix.

She—Mom, I mean—hasn't been normal lately. Even Aunt Dot thinks Mom is coming apart at the seams. That's what she told Mom. "Miriam, you're coming apart at the seams."

Mom has worn the same pair of jeans, the black ones with the holes in the knees, every day for a month, I'll bet. She says the holes are on purpose. So, I said, "What about the holes in the back, by the pockets?" She got really moody-like but didn't answer. Maybe they are because she has been eating a lot. Sometimes, when she's yelling at me, her mouth is full.

"Connie is my little helper," Mom tells Aunt Dot. I can see their reflection on the black TV screen. I'm in the family room and they're at the kitchen table. Aunt Dot is using both of her chubby hands to hold a coffee mug under her chins.

"I've been beside myself worrying about whether Henry is going to come through with the mortgage," Mom says.

Aunt Dot is Dad's sister, but she's not happy with him. "Hold his feet to the fire, Miriam. If he's got money enough to put up that little floozy girlfriend, he can pay the mortgage. It's the least he can do."

There's this girl in my class named Becky who had to go home sick one time. I heard the school nurse tell my teacher that Becky was "a little flu-zy." Becky isn't my girlfriend, though. Girls make me feel funny sometimes, and I get sweaty.

Mom reaches for the ginger molasses cookies that Aunt Dot brought over. They're my favorite. I want one so bad, but if I ask, Mom would say, "Not before breakfast, young man." I don't think she ate her breakfast yet.

They don't know I'm up. People usually don't notice me unless they're saying something about me that's wrong or needs to be fixed, like, when Mom says, "Get that hair out of your face." The barber says I have a nice head of black, baby-fine hair. "Unless I give the boy a crewcut, Miriam, it's going to eventually fall down his forehead." Mom says, "No crewcuts for you, Dell."

Dad notices me, too, but in a good way. He always squeezes one of my legs right above the knee until I yell, "I give!" It feels like I'm being electrocuted. At least, I think that's what it would feel like.

Sometimes, when I see him coming, I just yell, "I give!" so he won't do it. Then we watch TV together.

We like the cartoon shows and baseball. Me and Dad go to some Braves games. Just the two of us, but last year this lady met us at the stadium and sat with us a couple of times. Dad said they are friends. Then he winked at her. She had on lots of lipstick, and I sweated a little bit when she talked to me.

Right now, I'm sitting in the recliner—Dad's favorite seat—and it sort of feels like he's here. I'm pretending to be Dale Jr. at Daytona, working the chair lever like those NASCAR drivers shift gears.

I hear Mom sniffling again—she does that a lot when Aunt Dot is here—and I tiptoe over to the kitchen and peek in.

Mom's eyes look all soggy after she lifts her face out of her hands. She does this thing with her fingers, rubbing them through her hair, which is kinda two colors now—gray at the top and brown at the bottom. Usually, like in her wedding picture in the living room, it's brownie brown.

"It's all too stressful, Dot. I swear, if I didn't have Connie helping out and being a dear, I don't know what I'd do. It's like she understands what I'm going through and wants to help. Just this morning, before you came over, she washed and put away all of last night's dirty dishes and swept the kitchen."

Yeah, and last week, she snuck into my room and took one of my tennis shoes. I almost missed the school bus the next morning. The whole time, she was complaining to Mom, "Dell's gonna make us late again."

Mom could hear her but couldn't see Connie's snotty smile, the way she scrunched her nose up like she could smell a skunk. Her goony eyes opened really wide and she stuck her tongue out at me.

"Dell! I swear, you are the most disorganized kid," Mom yelled up the stairs. "Why can't you be more like your sister and less like your dad?"

Connie put a hand over her mouth, like she was gonna laugh out loud. Then, she turned her back to me and walked out of my room with her fingers pinching her nose. If I'd had that other shoe right then, I'd have thrown it at her fat head.

I wanna be like my dad. I even told Mom that, but she started crying again. Connie gave me a dirty look and said I was a stupid little kid.

When we got home from that camping trip last summer, Mom started asking how it went and did I have fun. I thought for sure Dad was gonna tell her what happened, but he didn't. And I'm pretty sure he never told Connie.

"He's quite the little outdoorsman," Dad told Mom, and I saw him wink.

Really, things aren't so bad between Connie and me when Dad is here. When I do something bad, he just raises an eyebrow and stares at me for a few seconds. He sticks up for me, too, the way Mom always sticks up for Connie. "He's just being a boy, Miriam," he says. I don't think Mom thinks I'm a boy anymore 'cause now, she says I have to be the man of the house. Connie laughed when she said it, but Mom frowned and said, "Connie, be nice."

My friend, Stilts, warned me, "Big sisters are the pits." Not sure how he knows that 'cause he doesn't have a sister. He doesn't have any brothers, either. If I didn't have a sister, Stilts told me, I'd probably get more presents at Christmas and on my birthday. Anyway, Stilts says I'm like his brother.

Connie hates Stilts. She says he's a freak. "What 9-year-old is that tall?"

Even though Stilts and me are the same age, he's 5 foot 10 already and I'm only 4 foot 8 if I wear my dress-up shoes. Mom says Stilts takes after his dad. His dad is pretty tall, even for a grownup. Both of them are kinda skinny and wear these big black glasses that are always sliding down their noses. Stilts says glasses make people look smart. I wonder if I look dumb 'cause I don't wear glasses.

I think I take after my dad, except when he takes off his Braves cap. I asked him if he was bald when he was my age. "When I was your age, we used to play Cowboys and Indians, and I got scalped," he said. He winked at me—he winks a lot—and then he put his Braves cap back on.

Being so tall is what makes Stilts smarter than me. He knows things I never even thought about. He says he knows when it's raining before I do. Or, like what he said about big sisters.

Stilts saw Connie skin the cat. Not, like, take a knife and scalp some alley cat. Skin the Cat is the name of a trick kids do, like acrobats. You have to hang upside-down from the top of a swing or some high place, with your arms hanging loose and everything.

Connie has been daring me to do it for a long time, calling me a chicken shit and other names. Oh, yeah, that's something else she does all the time that Mom doesn't know about—cuss. She—Connie, I mean—just wants to see me fall and crack my head open. I had this dream—I guess you'd call it a nightmare—and in it I fell trying to do the trick. Everybody was watching and laughing. I couldn't see who they were, because I was running home and on account of my eyes were all watery. My face felt so hot and snot was dripping from my nose.

I usually just give it right back to her, calling her a scaredy-cat, 'cause she couldn't do it either. But then Stilts came over with the bad news. He was delivering his newspapers when he saw Connie and her friends goofing around on a neighbor's swing. They have a really nice one. He watched from behind Mrs. Greeley's hedges so no one could see him. When he saw Connie skin the cat, Stilts dropped all the newspapers he had carefully folded and came running.

"Your sister skinned the cat!" he said. Not "hello" or "what's up" or anything like what two friends usually say. He was sucking in air really hard. "And worse, she had witnesses."

That was two days ago. Connie hasn't said anything, but she's smiling that sneaky smile every time we pass each other in the house. I know she's waiting for the perfect time to bring it up, like when Mom or Aunt Dot or some other grownup is around, to tell them how wonderful she is, and brave, and all that other crap. And me, of course. I'll just have to sit there and take it. It will be even more disgusting if one of the adults asks, "Isn't that something, Dell?"

At least I know what I have to do now. I've got to skin the cat, too. The sooner, the better. I tried to do it a couple of times, by myself, but I got scared and stopped. Now, all because Connie can do it, I'm gonna have to, too. If anything bad happens, like if I fall and break my neck and have to go to the hospital, it's all because of her. Like I said, she got me into this fix.

Summer didn't wait for school to be out this year. There's still a week to go and the zinnias Mom planted out in front of our house look sick and are crumbling up. She says they're "drought resistant," but I think they are half-dead. I give them extra water to drink whenever she's not around. The more water I give them, the worse they look. When Mom went to water them the last time, she scratched her two-color hair and said, "Huh? Still damp. That's strange."

I swallow the last gulp of Cap'n Crunch as I walk out onto the back porch on Saturday morning. My skin is already sticky under my new Braves T-shirt that Aunt Dot bought me from Target. I reach under my shorts and pull down on my underpants 'cause they're starting to scrunch up. Thinking about what I have to do today isn't helping, and I know I've got to do it before Connie gets up, or else she will be teasing me the whole time.

Our backyard is more dirt than grass. Mom says it's because Dad didn't take care of it. I know he will, though. He said this year he is gonna level the whole thing and plant new seeds. I'm gonna help him.

The yellow swing set sits on a patch of dust that goes a little downhill. There's just the one seat. It used to be bright red and shiny but now it looks sort of pink, and big chunks are peeling off. If somebody rocks back and forth just a little bit, the anchor poles will pop out of the ground six to eight inches. Stilts says they're supposed to be cemented into the ground. Doesn't matter 'cause the swing seat and chains aren't hooked up today.

Where is Stilts, anyway?

My nerves are so jumpy I can't stand still. I keep thinking about those three to four feet between the top of my head and the ground when I'm upside-down. What if I slip? What if I start daydreaming, like Mom says I do too much, and lose my concentration?

Even if I somehow do this trick, how in the heck am I gonna get down? That's as dangerous as doing the trick. It looks easy, the way I've seen other kids do it. You have to grab the bar again and do this sort of backwards somersault. All I can picture is my shoulders twisting right off, blood gushing from where they used to connect to my body.

Okay, think positive. You can do this.

As I'm telling myself that over and over, Stilts finally shows up, hopping off his bike and tossing it aside like he's jumping off a horse.

"What did I miss?" he asks.

"Where you been? And keep it down, please. If Connie or my Mom wake up and see me trying this, all hell is gonna break loose."

"Better 'all hell' than your neck," Stilts says, bursting out in his horse laugh.

Too late. Connie is at her bedroom window, yelling through the screen.

"Betcha can't do it, ya little sissy!"

I smile, try to act all cool, like I do this sort of thing every day. One thing is for sure, though. It's too late to back down now.

I can't get my hands all the way around the crossbar. That's gonna make it harder to do the trick. I might slip off 'cause there are rusty and loose paint chips all over it. When I try to hold on tight, it feels slippy-slidy underneath. And that's not all. Even though the sun has been up only about an hour, the crossbar is plenty hot already.

"Hey, Dumbo, better be careful. It's a long way down."

Just what I need, Connie teasing me when it's really important that I concentrate. Then, Stilts warns me about the chain mounts on the crossbar. "Those things can rip your hands to shreds."

Now, I'm thinking about jumping off the swing set and running. I don't know where I'd run to, but I'd run as fast and as far as I could, maybe to Alabama.

I don't know why, but my eyes are blurry all of a sudden. *Don't cry, don't cry.* I don't think I can do this. It feels just like when Dad wanted me to jump off that rock. It's like he's watching, and I'm gonna disappoint him again.

"Look at me, Dell," Stilts says. "Don't listen to her. You can do this."

I take as big a breath as I can and let it out really, really slow. Connie is still yapping behind the screen, like an angry bee when it's trapped in a jar, and Stilts is yelling for me to, "Go for it!"

Screw everything. I let go of the side bars and jump out to the middle with all my might. Only, I almost go too far. I get two hands on the crossbar, but my body keeps going. My legs whip out to the right and then whip back to the left. I'm like the flag at the stadium when the wind is blowing really hard.

"What are you doing, Dell?" Stilts calls out.

"I'm...trying...to...hang...on."

"Get a grip," he says, "and stop fooling around. You're almost there."

I'm getting a little dizzy. That makes me feel weak, but I get the back of one leg over the crossbar and, with the last drop of energy I have left, I get the other one over.

I did it! Stilts is jumping up and down and yelling, "Yes! Yes!" He really looks weird when you see him upside-down. *Oh my God, I'm upside-down.* "Stilts! Stop moving. You're making me sick to my stomach." I'm happy, but I'm dizzy at the same time.

"Goofball is gonna throw up!" Connie yells.

It feels like my body and my brain are confused. I might be falling, or am I just imagining it? I close my eyes as tight as I can, and then blink them really fast, hoping it will make everything stop.

It doesn't work. I'm getting dizzier. Upside-down Stilts is trying to warn me about something, but I can't hear any words now. Connie is pounding her fists on the window screen, but there is no sound, only this look on her face like she just made a horrible mistake.

Oh, God! I am falling!

But there isn't a great big boom! Instead, there is, like, this movie in my mind, and everything is happening in slow motion. I see my right leg straightening out, and I can't stop it. My left leg, which is all that is holding me on, slips off, too.

This is it! My shoulders squeeze together, and I expect to hear my skull crashing into the ground. Before that happens, though, I get this stupid thought: *Suicide is a mortal sin!*

I learned that at Religious Education. It's a class Mom makes us go to on Wednesday nights, even though we aren't really Catholics. She says it's a deal she made with Dad. We don't have to go to church, but we have to learn all that God stuff.

One of the first things they taught us, from a book called the Baltimore Catechism, was that if you kill yourself—on purpose, I mean—you're going to burn in hell for the rest of time.

What have I done!

Nobody made me do this except me. Okay, so Connie did in a way, and maybe Stilts pushed me a little bit.

Heck, who am I kidding?

This huge ball of dust goes up in the air when I crash into the ground. So much dirt is flying around my head that it is hard to see how I land. At the very last second, I must have turned my head just enough so that the side of my head and my shoulder are the first things to hit.

I thought it might sound like a pumpkin does when it smashes on the street, but it's more like a thud! Everything inside my head rattles and my ears pop. I can hear again—like, Connie's scream and Stilts, yelling, "Dell? Dell?" as he runs over to me.

"I killed myself!"

Oh, God! I didn't mean to do it. "I killed myself," I yell again as I get up, my knees all wobbly.

Connie is laughing. *So, this is what hell is like...Connie laughing at me all the time.*

"You're not dead, dumbass. You're walking." I hear her so clearly, and, even though she's up in the window, it sounds like, well, something in her voice, I think she's glad I'm still alive.

"Don't ever do that again, Dell," Stilts says. "You scared me for a second."

I'm not sure I believe I'm alive, but when I see Mom and Aunt Dot come out of the backdoor, grabbing for each other's hands and their mouths wide open, it feels like a railroad train zooms through my heart. I can't hold back. I start crying.

"What in the world is going on, Dell?" Mom says, putting her arms around me really tight. Then Aunt Dot says, "Ice. I'll get some ice."

I'm sobbing, and I point at the swing set. "I killed myself, Mom."

"I think you're going to live," Mom says as she stares up at Connie and then over at Stilts. "Your father should have gotten rid of that old thing years ago. It was just an accident waiting to happen."

I wipe at my eyes. "No, Mom. Dad's gonna fix it."

Aunt Dot comes out with some ice wrapped in a dish towel. Mom takes it from her but doesn't put it on my head right away.

"Dell, sweetie," she says, and takes a deep breath. "I don't think your dad's going to come back to fix it."

"He will, Mom. He's gonna fix it, and we're gonna plant new grass, and, you'll see."

Her voice is all trembly, but she isn't crying.

"Dell, you just have to understand," she says. "As much as you want it to be different, some things in life can't be fixed."

She takes my head and holds it so that I'm looking in her eyes. "But you know what? You're right. Sometimes, people hang on to things so hard that they forget they can replant and make something new."

"You mean, like the grass?" I ask, moving my head back against her stomach.

"Yes, like the grass, and like those flowers out front that don't seem to want to grow. I just need to pull them up and start over, maybe plant a different kind or pick a different spot."

For the first time after I fell from the crossbar, I believe I'm alive.

"Um, Mom? About those flowers."

Out of the Box

Mary Makofske

1921, and soldiers' arms and legs
lost in the war will not come home.
The audience is ripe for horror—
box like a coffin, metal blade,
a beautiful woman to saw in half—
as well as miracle, a woman whole
and smiling, emerging unscathed.
Practiced in illusion, she contorts
herself, imagines the thrill
she knows a few will feel
as the magician seems to sever
her lovely face from her nether parts.

A special thrill when the magician
is her husband, and the trick
bleeds over into real illusions
and restraints, or when Dorothy Dietrich
later reverses the roles and saws
her husband in two, slicing through
clichés, taking us out of the box.

Easy now to find the trick explained.
Too bad, because we love not knowing
how we've been deceived.
And still, as the blade descends,
the magician's assistant must
quail for a moment, the body imagined
under its stroke so tender, and we,
the audience, suspended in willing
disbelief, cut off from our usual values,
ourselves from ourselves, half-wishing
to see blood seep from the box to the floor.

ex tripudiīs *[from the "dance" (of birds feeding)]*

Devon Balwit

Each of us takes on the mantle of *pullarius*, observing
the chickens for auspices. Do they enter the house when the door
opens, or remain on the porch rail, squawking?
Do they come to our whistle or make it a chore

to retrieve them from the neighboring yards? A good appetite
means that democracy will prevail. Their ever-
increasing plumpness, that pandemic and partisan spite
will recede into the past like a boat wake in water.

We lift and loft them. How far can they still fly?
A good distance and we stop researching Canadian
citizenship. We strain our ears, trying
to divine the mood of the flock, panicky or Arcadian?

The chickens enjoy their office, and more than once
have made sport of us lumbering credulous humans.

Earwig Faces

Nathan Bas

There was an earwig trapped under a
flower pot, by one foot, where I set
the feet by design, just clumsily
doing what I do throughout my life.
It kept trying to escape the pot,
until it stopped—*or was it really?*—
I lift the pot, and it scurried away
as if fearful of a return journey.
Though, I wonder if animosity's
hidden by a lack of facial structure
and it's really charging some arrogance
of mine, hoping to lay eggs in my ears.
Who's to say? Just let it go do what it does
since it's similar to what you do all day.

Notes from a Portland Son

Scott F. Parker

I

They say Minneapolis is the first city of the West, but *they* always seem to be coming from the East. For Sandy and me, setting out from Portland, Minneapolis was the last place we could call "West."

We had planned to spend two years in Minnesota, but two turned into six, the way they can. Strangers became friends, friends became some of the dearest people to us in the world; and Oregon, season by season, started to take on a distinctly Edenic quality: an idea of a place we'd never return to. Favorite Twin Cities restaurants, walks by the lakes, neighborhood baristas who knew our names—we took root. By a considerable margin, six years was the longest we've lived in one place.

II

Sandy comes from a family of movers. Joining that long tradition of western optimism, she spent her childhood crisscrossing Wyoming at the call of her father's work (but breaking from the tradition, too, his career actually comprising a series of better jobs). Since Sandy left town after high school, her parents have gone on moving: to an unincorporated town in northern California, to suburban Oregon, and eventually to Texas hill country.

Mine, however, is a family of stayers. My mother has been a Portlander since she was among the first women to matriculate at Oregon Medical School (now OHSU), and my father has spent his days almost exclusively between Laurelhurst and Irvington. (For years he would cross the river only for his twice-weekly yoga class. Recently, he's improved upon that, finding a new class within walking distance.) The house they live in is the same one they bought when my mother was pregnant with me and there was still ash from Mount St. Helens in the gutter. My sister's house is a short bike ride away; and among cousins, aunts, and uncles, we've pretty much got the region covered from Corvallis to Olympia.

There's nothing unusual about this situation. If the West is a restless place—west of the West—the Northwest is to a meaningful degree a settled one. We are strangely dreamless about moving on, almost un-American in our contentedness to stay. Growing up, I never got the news that New York was the center of the universe. And a tropical paradise—Hawaii, say, or Mexico—was fine, but only for a week or so; any longer than that, let alone permanent, was seen as—everyone putting it this way—"a bit much." We had no California dreams—a quick look around the neighborhood revealed that everyone there was hurrying to get here. Only in college, when I started spending time with people who weren't from Oregon, did I first hear anyone complain about the rain. My understanding of *home* is colored by the fact that I grew up under the circumstance that the place everyone had wanted to get to had for proven itself in this case the place they wanted to be. There's no greener grass than what grows in the Willamette Valley.

Yet I left. Left Portland in the midst of one of those waves when so much of the rest of the country was arriving. The reasons weren't mythic or even romantic: no ricocheting off the Pacific with the momentum of progress behind me. Such ambitions simply never arose.

Why would they? Where I grew up, *progress* was synonymous with *history*—it had served its purpose. When I left, it was for the ordinary reasons: opportunities and commitments: grad school for Sandy, an itinerant writing life for me.

But very few of my childhood friends did leave Portland. Of those who did, it's obvious in retrospect that some of them needed to (even if no one said so at the time). Others of us might easily have stayed and were merely lucky to leave. What I'm calling luck here was for me the chance to find out that lush as the gardens are, Oregon only becomes Eden from a remove.

Nevertheless, two or three times a year I make the trip back to Portland, trying to prove I never left, or maybe play around with the possibility that I never did. In these six years, neither Sandy nor I got around to replacing our Oregon driver's licenses.

III

Minneapolis never looked so much like an oasis in the prairie as when I watched it recede in the sideview mirror of the U-Haul as I merged on to I–94 and started back west with most of Minnesota and too much North Dakota ahead of me.

West of Fargo, I watched the sun set like a falling target. Sandy was in our car with our cat, who hadn't taken food or water all day, as I followed in the truck hellbent on Bismarck, where we had a reservation. We pulled in sometime after midnight. The hotel was at capacity, stuffed like a barrack with oil workers down from the Bakken. The parking lot was an advertisement for high-end white pickups. I parked the U-Haul a block away and nodded to the oversized men I passed. They were intoxicated, if not chemically then with the rush of dreams part-way fulfilled. Their trucks were expensive, the hotel was expensive, and as long as oil prices stayed high, they could afford it a lot easier than we could. When life is good, it's natural to think it always will be. The current boom had already crested, but here we all were in Bismarck for the time being.

Our ultimate goal was Bozeman, where we were headed not by choice but by good fortune: a computer algorithm had declared that Sandy's new job would be at Montana State University. We were woebegone to be leaving our friends in Minnesota, but we were optimistic for Bozeman, which had recently developed a reputation as a "destination city" and was (unfortunately for our rent) undergoing a real estate boom of its own. What was at work here? Another fantasy of the West? One that might be fulfilled? For us: a quick stopover on our return trip to Portland or somewhere we might settle even longer than the six years of Minneapolis? We didn't know what we'd find in Montana or how long we'd stay, but by the time we arrived our cat had finally taken a sip of water, and as we unloaded the U-Haul it felt like we might be halfway home.

Departure

Peter Vertacnik

He's lived two decades in this house
And can't believe he has to leave.
It makes him want to have a drink
While he sits waiting for the sun
To light the branches of the elder.
His thoughts attempt to light the past.

Yet he knows dwelling on what's passed
This final morning in the house
Is selfish. Staring at the elder
Won't change the fact they have to leave,
Or help console his wife and son.
He knows this. Still, he'd like a drink.

Just one, he thinks, *just a small drink—*
Enough to help him make it past
This next hour when he's sure his son,
Stomping through the empty house,
Will scream, "Why do we have to leave?"
The boy reminds him of his elder

Brother, who'd sit beneath the elder
With him each Saturday and drink
Those anxious weeks he was on leave,
Though since then twenty years have passed.
There was one phone call to the house
That August, just before his son

Was born, but nothing more...The sun
Spreads swiftly now between the elder
Leaves as it climbs the waking house.
There's no time left for one last drink,
No time to clarify the past.
He'll tell his son, "It's time to leave,

That's why, because it's time to leave,"
And then turn in the glaring sun
As from a test he hasn't passed.
He'll never lean against the elder
Again, enjoying a cold drink;
Or sit here thinking in this house

About the past. Knowing both elder
And house are lost, he needs a drink.
But he, his wife, and son must leave.

Homage to Telesilla of Argos
(fl. 500 bce), Port Largo

—*philêlias*, hymn to Apollo; *oupingoì*, hymn to Artemis.

Ricardo Pau-Llosa

A week away from the sea and my canal,
and the house repairs across the way are done.
In the house next to that one, with the banal
tuna on the canal-side wall, the garden
has been worked, the golden palms shorn
of frazzle and ripe coconuts, the tiki varnished.
I glimpse the gleam of new paint on the worn
hoisted hulls, the buoys tied and bleached.
The teak dining set honeyed by stain
has shed the silver weather had inscribed.
Fall's the proper time—cool, less rain—
to ready homes for visits from the tribe
of cast familiars, to revel in calendar's end,
although here all year one season reigns.

Behold how the copters spraying for mosquitoes cross
Largo in bands, south to north, their grey
plumes floating west in the winds that toss
fronds into waves. And although the bright day
is ideal for sailing, all the boats are still,

and the only motors I hear are overhead.

Shoals which travel currents to follow krill

let the fishermen sleep. The ocean's herds

have set their clocks. Hunter and prey hear

what each must to cue their urgency.

For none that live are starved of fear,

and none can drown time's poison melody.

The goddess sings to call her golden hind,

the silver tarpon, and the bronze hawk to mind.

Thank You (It Might Have Been Otherwise)

—after W.S. Merwin and Jane Kenyon

Mary Rohrer-Dann

Listen
for the brief slow soundless dream into green
the blessed blank of oblivion then
and now I am saying thank you
it might have been otherwise
for responders' black boots upside-
down, resolute by the windshield
for voices calling calmly to me
I am saying thank you, it might
have been otherwise

for the thrum of blades above me
soft air buffeting my face
and the thought bright as a struck bell
this is my first helicopter ride?
I am saying thank you
it might have been otherwise

for the trauma room P.A., her face
inches from mine, her eyes
holding mine, her kind voice telling me

what had happened, what was happening
what would happen, making me feel safe
and I said and I am saying thank you
it might have been otherwise

for fractured cervical bones, sternum, ribs,
and lower spine, but no surgery, no paralysis,
just a three-day hospital stay (and the words
over and over chanting in my brain
I sing the body electric) I am saying
thank you thank you, I know how easily
it might have been otherwise

for the small brain bleed, the hand laceration
that a year later are only ephemeral
dizziness, a barely-there scar, I am saying
thank you, it might have been otherwise

for my husband and my daughter
—there are no accurate words—
I am saying thank you, thank you
for all my family and friends
near and far their words and prayers
visits and meals and chocolates and books
phone calls and texts and beautiful cards,
and so many flowers and so much love
for all these I am saying thank you thank you

And for my tough fragile resilient body
so fleeting and miraculous
still magnificently carrying me through
I am saying thank you
I am saying thank you
I am saying thank you

Elegy for a Stranger

Alanna Weissman

Dearly departed, I'm sorry I never knew you. We might have passed each other on the way to work, stood next to each other on a crowded train, our elbows brushing with each bump of the rail. Maybe you washed my hair at a salon, and I apologized for my split ends and the grease built up at my roots. Or maybe you served me my food at a trendy new restaurant, or scanned my groceries when they reached the end of the conveyor belt. We might have favored the same market because it was the only one that carried a particular type of olives, or because it somehow sold summer peaches year-round, or because the shelves were always stocked just so. Perhaps I stood in line behind you at the checkout counter as you counted your change and silently complimented your clothes, wishing I could pull off a style like that. Maybe I watched you run laps at the park and admired your form and endurance; maybe you stopped to tie your shoe on the bench where I sat. Or maybe we crossed paths at the same local dive, made small talk about the weather, had a furtive hookup in the bathroom, our breath hot on each other's faces, and didn't exchange numbers afterward. The same apps on our phones might have pinged off each other when we were in proximity. We might have been in the audience together at a concert, the crowd moving as one to the thrum of our favorite song. Or I might have seen you in an internet video playing a guitar or a keyboard or a ukulele, a small attempt at fame. We might have unknowingly appeared in the backgrounds of each other's photos, our arms slung over our friends' shoulders, captured forever in place. Perhaps you lived across the way, knocked on my door once to give me a piece of mistakenly delivered mail because we had similar names. Maybe we watched the same TV show, our screens displaying the images in perfect sync. Maybe I saw you sitting on your fire escape in a bathrobe sipping coffee (or was it tea?) out of a blue mug just like the one my mother gave me when I moved out. Maybe I glimpsed you through a windowpane as you smoothed your daughter's hair and tucked her into bed, watched your lips move soundlessly curling upward at the edges, noticed the tenderness of your hands as they lingered on the wall before flicking off the light switch.

Dearly beloved, I can feel your presence lingering in the air, the molecules still vibrating. Perhaps we would not have even liked each other; maybe your hates were my loves. Perhaps we never would have crossed paths at all. But water from the same earth flowed over our hands and bodies, the same air expanded in our lungs. The same sunlight glittered on our skin; our reflections moved transient on the same surfaces. Our flattened shadows silhouetted on the same ground, sometimes taller than us, sometimes shorter. Even if it didn't feel like it—some years faster, some slower—time passed the same for both of us. The muscles in our faces knew the same movements—of joy, of anger, of surprise, of sorrow. We have all felt. We have all lost. You will be missed.

Speaking from the Winter of My Life

Diane Averill

There is an energy
still moving along the rivers of my bloodstream
in continuous cycles.
My stream of life is long. I may seem just
an old woman, but inside dreams are young and
young dreams are tenacious, don't die easily.

Now, in winter, I follow their energy in a different way,
along icy stream beds, finding all
flowing water beautiful
especially at night, swimming in oceans of stars
that have no end, their light traveling
currents of galaxies into infinity.

So what do I really know?
Only that everyone's lives are matter made from
our ancestors' dreams,
infused together in nerves and veins and organs,
and in slow contemplations over sweet teas.

All Over Again

Melissa McKinstry

It's Christmas, and last night I dreamed again
of you talking and walking.

You toddled toward me with a huge smile,
open arms, and chirped "Mama!"

like I was a prize. What I thought was a miracle
turned out to be that dream again.

What I thought was healing turned out to be sick regret
from my subliminal mind—that old trickster.

What I thought was a whole different life for you
and for me, turned out to be, upon waking,

the same life we've been living for 23 years—
oxygen concentrator burrs, heart monitor beeps,

and the food pump announces *dose delivered*
all over again, even as the red crepe myrtle sifts the rain.

The Masked Daughter

William J. Cobb

It's late afternoon and I'm in a Zoom meeting at my desk upstairs, sitting in front of the window so the light falls on my face for the video feed, ignoring the laptop screen in front of me, staring out at our mountainside yard—white fir and golden aspen leaves against a blue sky—watching my daughter and her friend Haley perched on top of her redwood play-fort, high up in the air, when Indi pushes her friend off the roof.

I'm not really paying attention to the Zoom or Indi and her friend until then. My colleague Anita is ranting about a scheduling issue with her classes and then—behind her, behind the laptop screen that holds the images of my Zoom participants, like a rip in the fabric of reality—there's the real world, with Indi and Haley perched like cut-out dolls on the play-fort roof. Aspens on one side of the fort, their white trunks with black knots shaped like Cleopatra's eye makeup, their gold and yellow wobbling leaves. Fir trees on the other side. One second the girls are sitting together, both facing east, with Haley at the edge. Then Indi shoves her. Haley vanishes into the air. Indi scoots forward and looks down. She stares below her for a moment, glances back at the house—where she can't see me, hidden behind the sunlight reflection on the windows—and starts to climb down from the roof, choosing her footholds carefully.

I click the video off and rush outside.

Haley sits in the fine dirt beneath the swing set, where she fell, looking stunned. Her nose is bleeding, and she has her head down. Fat red drops of blood speckle her white Vans sneakers. Indi crouches beside her, petting her hair and cooing, telling her how sorry she is. The air smells of microwave popcorn—one of the few things Indi will now eat. Before they climbed to the playfort roof, they'd been watching a recording of *The Masked Singer*, their latest obsession. They eat microwave popcorn and watch the cheesy reality show. It's a thing.

"I didn't mean it," she says, parting Haley's red and blue hair with her fingertips. "I was just joshing you and then you were, like, in the air!"

"Mean what?" asks Haley.

Indi pauses, brushing the dirt off Haley's forehead. She leans over and kisses her scalp. "Are you okay? I mean, you're not hurt are you?"

Haley winces, breathing with her mouth open. She's sitting at an odd angle—her head crooked on her neck—holding her right wrist with her left hand. Indi pulls the hood of her sweatshirt over her head, as if trying to hide. Teardrops dribble down Haley's pink cheek. "My arm," she says. She has dirt and aspen leaves in her hair. Indi starts picking at them and telling her everything's going to be okay. She looks at me and says, "She just fell. The craziest thing. We were sitting there, and she just fell."

Haley winces and says it hurts. Below her wrist the skin bulges out.

"It's not broken, is it?" asks Indi. "Oh frickin' Jesus tell me it's not broken."

I tell her it might be. I don't know. And don't say *frickin'*. "I'll go get the car keys and we'll all go to the clinic to see."

"My parents are going to kill me," says Haley. Her face is streaked with reddish brown dirt and tears. "They don't have insurance or anything."

I tell her it's okay. I'll cover it.

We lay her back beneath the swing-set. It's windy and their chains squeak as they sway. I run to the house and grab a box of Kleenex, run back, and tear off a piece, twist it into a little ball, and have Haley push it up her nose. She lies there in the dirt, mouth agape like a carp, with a blue Kleenex twirl hanging from her nose.

When my daughter is with her friends, it's hard to tell them apart, hard to know which is which. They all wear masks now when they're out in public—or at least when parents are around and they're pretending to be "good." They wear masks and hoodies, so you can't see much of their faces. All their ninth-grade classes are online, and when you see Zoom feeds of them as a group, it's really hard to tell one from another. They're just pixels on a screen—interchangeable, the screen icons rearranging automatically when one drops out, another pops up. It's hard to recognize them as actual kids. They're just confusing *simulacra*, often in shadows, as they Zoom from their beds or a corner of the den, with tennis rackets and dart boards in the background.

Haley is the better-student half of this BFF duo. She loves school and does her assignments ahead of time, makes straight A's, the Honor Roll. Her mother, a rather frazzled woman named Victoria, is an irritating Karen type, who constantly humble-brags about how well Haley is doing in her classes, how all the other kids resent her. Haley is also a star on the tennis team. Indi struggles to dribble a basketball if I twist her arm and bribe her into playing a game of Horse. When I take snapshots of them together Haley always smiles wide and bright, showing all her teeth, while Indi stares blankly with a fashion-model pout.

We live in a nice neighborhood on the slopes of Cheyenne Mountain, yards full of aspens and evergreens, basketball hoops in the driveways. Our backyard is fenced, and that's where Haley and Indi like to hang out on top of Indi's play-fort, which I built for her when she was six years old: A two-story redwood playset with a peaked roof including a tiny dormer window (which once harbored a wasp nest), a swing-set off to one side, a green plastic side on the other. The slide always seems to have a puddle of murky water at the bottom, where it flattens out. They climb onto the roof by standing at the top of the slide and using the roof beams for foot holds. It's where Indi likes to brood. Mainly she listens to rap music and stares at her phone.

They all do. Haley and Indi and Kiwi. Kiwi's real name is Caitlin but everyone calls her Kiwi, due to her obsession with New Zealand. That's where she's going to live when she gets out of college, she told Indi. She's a tiny girl with wavy black hair and paper-white skin. She basically doesn't talk to me directly. If I speak or ask her a question, she'll whisper to Indi, who acts as her interpreter and spokesperson. When I first learned her real name was Caitlin I smiled and said, "Caitlin's a pretty name. I bet your parents call you Katie."

She leaned close to Indi and whispered. Indi grinned and said, "Really?"

"So did they call her Katie?" I ask.

"Kiwi says 'They used to. Not anymore.'"

"Why not?"

"She says she told them if they ever did so again, she'd walk into the path of a speeding pickup truck."

I asked how her parents responded. Kiwi bent close to Indi again and whispered. "Kiwi says her parents said, 'Okay.'"

In our Ford Bronco Haley lies prone in the back seat, her head in Indi's lap. Indi keeps petting her hair and Haley breathes with her mouth open, telling us her head hurts, too. The clinic is a fifteen-minute drive and Indi refuses to wear the shoulder strap because it would go across Haley's face and I'm like fine whatever. The clinic is in a strip mall, and we have to scramble around in the car to find face masks for all of us before we go in. Haley is still breathing with her mouth open and acts like the mask is choking her.

"I can't breathe," she whines, crying.

After we check in Haley and Indi sit across from me, in the plastic chairs, staring at their iPhones and texting. They take a selfie with their masked faces pressed together and post it on Instagram. Haley texts her Mom, who works at Trader Joe's, telling her what's going on. After a while I get a text from her and I tell her I don't really know what happened. I was in the house and the girls were on the play-fort. I shouldn't have let them hang out there, I admit.

Victoria charges into the clinic with a stern face and frizzy hair, a black face mask with the legend **Mansplain Free Zone**. "So, they were up on a roof, is that what you're telling me?"

I admit that's the truth.

"And what made Haley fall?"

"I don't know," I tell her. "I wasn't there. I was inside the house on a zoom call. India came to get me, telling me Haley was hurt."

"She just slipped and fell?" says Indi. "The craziest thing."

Victoria stares at Indi. She once told me she can smell a lie a mile away. The lines on her forehead tense and contract. "How did she slip? Wasn't she sitting down?"

Indi looks down at her phone and shrugs, says, "I'm not sure. I wasn't really like watching her, you know what I mean? And all the sudden I heard this like loud thunk and there she was, on the ground and everything."

"Why weren't you watching?"

"I was texting Kiwi about *The Masked Singer.* We just watched a new episode." She smiles mischievously. "I think I know who the Honey Badger is."

All of them are obsessed with this stupid Fox TV show, *The Masked Singer.* B-list celebrity goons wear ridiculous costumes and prance around singing cover songs of pop hits, judged by other pop-music celebrity stooges. The whole thing is a farce, but the girls love it. They say it's so uncool it's cool.

Kiwi appears in the hospital-room doorway, as if summoned by emo spirit-wish power. Victoria squirts hand sanitizer into her palms and Kiwi stands there, a tiny little thing rubbing her hands together, wavy black hair covering half her face. She looks at Haley in the hospital bed and mime's sadness, rubs imaginary tears from her eyes. "How's the victim of the tragic accident?" she whispers.

"I'm alive," says Haley. "As if you care."

Victoria frowns. "Is that any way to greet your friend? What's got into you?"

Haley rolls her eyes. "Is that what she is, a friend?"

Actually, Kiwi and Haley don't really like each other. Kiwi is Indi's girlfriend girlfriend, while Haley is her BFF. It's obvious they're rivals, but usually the drama plays out behind the scenes, like when they went trick-or-treating last year and Haley wore this *Lord of the Rings* costume—as Arwen, the princess played by Liv Tyler—with a sexy dress and pointed ears. Haley said Kiwi looked like some kind of elf whore. "I mean, in a good way," she added.

Indi announced she was Bi in the seventh grade, right around the time she and Meghan, my wife, started fighting over her taste in macabre cosmetics. Indi is semi-Goth, semi-Egyptian: Like Cleopatra at a Horror Con Film Fest. She follows gay makeup gurus on Youtube, Instagram and TikTok, who appear to live high-drama lives. Indi is all drama herself, and her eyes show it. Purple eye shadow and black eyeliner, mascara to make her lashes black and spikey.

Meghan and I, we don't fret about her girlfriends. Honestly, we're just glad she's avoiding boys.

Kiwi corrects your pronunciation if you vary from accepted usage. Somehow, we were once talking about how her middle-school teacher was so conservative she was acting like Charles Darwin was a kook, and I said something about evolution. Kiwi glanced at me and leaned close to Indi.

"Kiwi says it's pronounced eh-volution, not ee-volution," she told me.

"Well," I explained, "the Oxford English Dictionary, or O.E.D. as it's known, lists 'ee-volution' as the first choice. Brits tend to say 'ee-volution,' while Americans tend to say 'eh-volution.'"

Kiwi looked unconvinced. She leaned forward and whispered in Indi's ear. Her lips were practically touching Indi's earlobe.

"Kiwi asks what country we're in right now," said Indi, smiling.

I explain that I like the long vowel sound of 'ee-volution.'

"Kiwi thinks words should not be a matter of like and dislike," said Indi, after another consultation.

I looked up at the ceiling and sighed, searching for help from God, perhaps, or just patience. "Perhaps," I suggested, "Kiwi's thinking will 'ee-volve' with time."

"I'm right here," said Kiwi, softly, putting her head on Indi's shoulders. "You don't have to pretend I'm not."

My wife, Meghan, arrives at the hospital, carrying a dozen roses and a box of Dunkin donuts, wearing an orange and yellow tie-dye mask. She's all about yoga and mindfulness. I call her my Hippie Wife and love her for not being like Victoria—who has her secrets, no doubt, though I doubt they involve lingerie.

I don't say a word to Meghan about seeing Indi push Haley off the playhouse roof.

In the hospital hallway the next day I have to push Indi toward Haley's room. She's claiming disaster fatigue. With the election coming up and all, she's worn out. "I'm tired of living through historical events," she whines. She's been telling me how bad she feels and how Haley won't forgive her ever again. I stand behind her and give her a little nudge. "Come on. Face the music."

She shuffles in the doorway like a defendant into the court-room for arraignment. The room is dim with the curtains half-drawn, and smells of flowers, two big vases on the end table, a gaggle of balloons tied to the bedframe, lurid with Get Well Soon written in neon script.

Victoria says "Hello" and turns away as soon as we enter, saying, "Look, Muffin. India is here to see you again."

Haley barely glances up from her phone. "Hey." She narrows her eyes at Indi. "What did you bring me?"

Indi's arms are hidden behind her back. She's wearing a red face mask emblazoned with **Hopeless Case**. "Bring you? Like I'm supposed to bring you something?"

Haley nods. "Them's the rules." She pushes her bangs down over her face, trying to suppress a little smile. "It's in the manual."

"What manual?"

"The victim-of-a-fall manual." They're both smiling now. Victoria is reading a hardback titled *The President Is Missing*. She doesn't look up or acknowledge me. Her hair looks even shorter and spikier than usual. Like someone hooked up jumper cables to Frankenstein's wife.

"Sorry, Charlie," says Indi. "I got a whole lotta nothin'."

"Then what's that behind your back?"

"I'm not holding anything," says Indi. She backs up until she's leaning against the windowsill and scoots her butt against it, then pulls out both hands, empty. "See?"

"You don't love me anymore, do you, Heathcliff?" says Haley, in a British accent.

Indi swoons and falls across the bed, upsetting everything. With them, this is a Thing: They fall all over each other every chance they get, run up to each other and hug and fall to the ground even if they've just seen each other the day before. It's violent and silly and they love it. When Indi falls on the bed, she knocks Haley's breakfast tray to the side, simultaneously pulling a stuffed animal out from behind her and pushing it into Haley's face, making kissy noises. "You mean this?"

Victoria frowns and picks the tray off the floor. "Girls? Could you be more careful?"

Haley grins at Indi, rubbing her nose against the beak of the stuffed animal. "For me?"

Indi nods. "Introducing Aquatica Mortimer, Emperor Penguin extraordinaire! Soon to be a contestant on..."

Haley grins. "The Masked Singer?"

"You guessed it! For that you receive a prize of…"

"A lifetime supply of Eskimo Pies?"

Indi frowns. "Eskimo pies? That is so *inappro*, I don't know where to begin."

"Inuit pies then?"

"What say we go with Indigenous People's Pies?"

"Ugh. That's a mouthful."

Then they both laugh like crazy.

What complicates this scenario is that Indi and Haley claim they're gay, or bi, and their girlfriends, but they're not, too. They're not girlfriends girlfriends, if that makes any sense. They're friends and rivals and text constantly and who knows what in their secret moments, which they have lots of.

Victoria points out that Haley has to stay for two nights for observation, due to her concussion). She won't look at me when she speaks. She's like an angry Karen ready to call the cops.

I tell her I'm sorry. *We're* sorry. "I shouldn't have let them go up on the roof, I know."

She nods. "Yes, well. These things happen, I guess. Especially when we're not watching what's going on."

Haley and Indi take a selfie together, with Indi scrunching up on the bed beside Haley and maneuvering her iPhone into position. Indi smiles wide and Haley keeps her mouth closed, looking petulant, which is a change for her. Then she tells us how much she hates the hospital and everyone in it.

"Isn't the air in here dead?" she asks. "I feel like I'm in a frickin' morgue."

Victoria stands at the window, staring out, her back to us. "Haley? Since when is *frickin'* good English?"

Haley rolls her eyes and gives her mother the finger behind her back. She's showing off for Indi. "Who cares about good English?" she asks. "I'm in the *frickin'* hospital. By the way," adds Haley. "Have you stabbed the President yet?"

Indi grins and shakes her head, causing her red and blue hair to swirl around. "No, but it's only a matter of time."

Indi, the Woke thing that she is, hates the President, and often describes how she would like to kill him. It often involves stabbing him, usually with a jagged piece of broken mirror (the symbolism, get it?) but running him over with a monster truck or tossing him in a meat grinder are also popular choices. Meghan and I try to tamp down her murderous impulses. "Is it a good idea to talk about stabbing people?" we asked. "Or assassinating the President? People could get the wrong idea."

"I'll just do it and not talk about it." She then went on to describe how she'd like to gouge out his eyeballs.

"Indi? Enough already. And whatever you do, don't talk about politics or the upcoming election with strangers."

Why? She asked.

"For one thing, you might get shot," said Meghan.

The next morning, we wake to find Indi fussing in the kitchen, her hair twisted into a wacky ponytail flip on top of her head. She's cheery and has already made a pot of coffee in the French press, set the table with napkins and plates. She's wearing a black crop top and sweatpants, telling us all about some girl named Stella Abernathy, who is a serious Thirst Trap on TikTok but she can't stand her. "Such a phony," she says. "You wouldn't believe it. She's like a bad algebra problem: Basic Girl Squared."

She pours Meghan's coffee in the white mug she made in the fifth grade, a birthday present, that has **Best Mom in the World!** painted in red slashes. On the kitchen table she places three brightly colored Fiestaware plates, fries eggs and bacon for us, and has yogurt with granola (she's vegetarian).

Meghan smiles at the food and the table. "Has there been a kidnapping?"

Indi grins, cocks her head sideways, making the hair flip droop to one side. "Why, pray tell?" Acting like some movie-daughter she saw on the screen somewhere.

"My daughter has never made me breakfast before," explains Meghan. "So, she must have been kidnapped and replaced by a clever copy."

"Oh, geez, Mom," she says, rolling her eyes. "What's such a big deal about it?"

"Plus, usually you're in bed all morning," I add.

"Well maybe I shouldn't be sleeping my life away, now should I?"

"That's what I always say."

"Well," she pauses dramatically, standing beside the table, pouring orange juice into our glasses. "Maybe you're right."

"I'm always right," I say.

"Uh huh, right," she says, sarcastically, then starts telling us all the news she's read on her laptop this morning. "Did you hear that one of the big California wildfires was caused by a gender-reveal party color-bomb explosion?" she adds. "That's so cray-cray! I mean, like, isn't the gender-reveal hoopla sheer madness. Especially, like, now? I mean, get on the bus or you'll miss the field trip. Aren't we all fluid now?"

"Maybe *you're* all fluid now. I'm a solid."

She opens her mouth and emits a silent laugh, eyes squinched shut. "But really, who knows who is who anymore? Gender reveals are so retro. It's like begging for a do-over. Let's reveal it's a boy now and then it's a she later! Will there be another party? Burn down another state?"

Meghan agrees with Indi. "You can't even tell a who from a what anymore."

"Or a which," I add.

"You mean witch? Like with brooms and shit?" asks Indi.

"Did you say, 'bosoms' and shit?"

"Brooms and shit!"

"Language?" says Meghan. "Since when is it okay to cuss at breakfast?"

Indi laughs. "Since I got up early and made it, maybe?"

"Touché," I add. "Next thing I know, you'll be a Vsco-girl."

"Never," says Indi, making a gagging motion—finger in mouth. "But that's so over. Now it's all about Basic Girls and Thirst Traps, which are exclusive, by the way, as in one does not mix with the other."

"What's a thirst trap?"

She sighs. "Where to begin?"

I put on a look of mock confusion. "Am I getting behind in the lingo?"

"No, Dad. You're not *getting* behind. You're just *behind*."

While Haley recovers at home, Indi spends the afternoons after her online zoom classes playing tennis with Kiwi at the park down the street, where she used to sit beneath the aspens and make fun of all the peppy, sporty kids. Now she's one of them. She gives herself a pageboy haircut and takes to wearing pleated white tennis skirts, which she had never done before. When I ask her how Haley is doing, Victoria quits answering my texts. Once I see her in the Trader Joe's parking lot and wave. She doesn't respond. I think she's pretending that she didn't see me, but I know she did. First the kids, now the Moms: Soon I'll be completely invisible, pretend-wise.

I keep thinking I should tell Meghan how Indi pushed Haley off the roof. But I don't. She wants to believe Indi has turned a corner. She's so excited when Indi tells us she's trying out for the tennis team, first thing, after the pandemic ends. Meghan was on the tennis team at the UC Boulder, said it was her favorite thing about college. "You'll be just like me," she tells Indi. And her daughter actually smiles.

When grades are reported after the six-week marking period, Indi has all As, first time ever. We buy her a skateboard and she takes off down the street, making that clockety-clock noise, like a natural. A car honks and we frown at them when they pass, and at the last second, I realize it's Victoria. When Indi comes home, she's glowing, and thanks both of us, giving us hugs and cheek kisses. With her new mask on—a black one that says Hopeless Case, just like Haley's—she looks like Haley's twin now. Without the arm in a cast.

After dinner we take our places around the flat screen to watch the season finale of *The Masked Singer*. "It's the big reveal!" squeals Indi. "I can't wait."

I tell her it doesn't matter. We all wear masks now, don't we?

Kids Have No Place

Jeffrey Kingman

dew point, decimal off quotidian
back, librarian will find reunite
kiss corner Westerns L'Amour
burning nipples nape *mine yours, let's—*
bookshelver   shit

flip-flop to local documents
slapfeet too loud
reference no good
sneak stall in women's
he feet on toilet she
grabs waist lip nipple—
too no!
"Young lady..."
security boots

but somewhere brightness
will be arranged
voices replaced
time

well, just be
maybe up
or at
something quiet

Saint-Didier-La-Forét

Andrew Rader Hanson

Each bead of sweat
　　slakes the crisp brush
beneath our feet
　　and when the night cools
day from the summer's
　　flame to its Sapphic blue
source, and finally to black,
　　pale portraits
of ancestors, eminent
　　men and women, swathe
the walls and watch
　　as our drinks clink dry.

Communion

Meli Broderick Eaton

Placed
as I am here
a ghost housed
like an egg nested
deep in mangroves inside
the chaos of vessels and sinew
of bone and sponge where blood runs
at the speed of life

given
this gift of breath
I am to learn to see
other miracles that breathe
and fly and sway and tower tall
I feel the weighted pull of obligation
to feast the eyes until memory is bursting
with the color of living

brief

this time to commune

with the rattle and thrust

of seed pods pushed by new life

of indigo night cracked open by light

the wind strumming through pine needles

like a lover's fingers and this is how I know

a tree can feel love

wondering

mind wandering heart

each beat one closer to last

I could run so fast I leave myself

far behind never on time but following

if I ever catch up time will have already

caught up to me and I am back among the stars

blinking my astonishment

A Magnificent Gauze

Mark Simpson

Just before I fell asleep on the train from Beginning to End
(or was it from New to Old? I've traveled so much these years I forget)
a man sat next to me who smoked cigars.

I could tell from the smell. A businessman, I guessed, in those clothes
they wear, tweed and tie and matching slacks and shoes that almost
shined but did not. That is to say I could smell the smoke—
Cuban or Kentuckian, one of the two.

And as I dozed I imagined how he cupped one hand around the light
the other held and then the smoke, a magnificent gauze
that mixed the apparent and real, in the way caught fish flop in the hold
of a boat. I half woke, then dozed again.

All things are half probable in dreams on trains.
All things seem stations on the way, known and forgettable, half noticed
in the way trains sway through countryside and city.
When I awoke he was still there, the man of smoke and half-shined
        shoes,
asleep, a folded newspaper in his lap. Night was coming on.
Or was it day?

Contributors

Ken Autrey is Professor Emeritus of English at Francis Marion University and now lives in Auburn, Alabama. His work has appeared in *Atlanta Review*, *Cimarron Review*, *Poetry Northwest*, *Southern Poetry Review*, *Texas Review*, and elsewhere. He has published three chapbooks: *Pilgrim* (Main Street Rag), *Rope Lesson* (Longleaf Press), and *The Wake of the Year* (Solomon and George). He is a coordinator of the Third Thursday Poetry Reading Series at Auburn University.

Diane Averill's books, *Branches Doubled Over With Fruit*, published by the University of Florida Press, and *Beautiful Obstacles*, published by Blue Light Press of Iowa, were finalists for the Oregon Book Award in Poetry. She has had two other books and three chapbooks published since then. Her poems appear in literary magazines around the country, and in Great Britain. Her work appears in magazines such as *The Bitter Oleander*, *CALYX*, *Clackamas Literary Review*, *CIRQUE*, and *Poetry Northwest*. Diane holds an M.F.A degree from The University of Oregon and taught at Clackamas Community College until her retirement.

When not teaching, **Devon Balwit** chases chickens in Portland, OR, USA. Her individual poems can be found in *The Worcester Review*, *The Cincinnati Review*, *Tampa Review*, *Barrow Street*, *Tar River Poetry*, *Clackamas Literary Review*, *Rattle*, *Bellingham Review*, and *Grist*, among others. Her most recent chapbook is *Rubbing Shoulders with the Greats* [Seven Kitchens Press, 2020].

Nathan Bas is a Clackamas Community College alumnus living in Oregon City, Oregon, currently studying Creative Writing and English at Portland State University, with publications in *Polaris* and *Clackamas Literary Review*. He once had a passing whim to drop everything and live in the forest to write eccentric gibberish, but the likelihood of death, via thirst or cougar, was a deal-breaker. Now he spends moderately undue proportions of Christmas and birthday money on houseplants to create his own indoor jungle.

Trent Busch, a native of rural West Virginia, now lives in Georgia where he writes and makes furniture. His recent books of poetry, *not one bit of this is your fault* (2019) and *Plumb Level and Square* (2020) were published by Cyberwit.net. His poems have appeared in *Best American Poetry*, *Poetry*, *The Nation*, *Threepenny Review*, *North American Review*, *Chicago Review*, *Southern Review*, *Georgia Review*, *New England Review*, *Crazyhorse*, *Prairie Schooner*, *Northwest Review*, *Kenyon Review*, *American Scholar*, *Shenandoah*, *Boston Review*, and *Hudson Review*. His poem "Edges of Roads" was the 2016 First Place winner of the Margaret Reid Poetry Prize.

William J. Cobb is a novelist, short story writer, and essayist whose work has been published in *The New Yorker* and many other journals. His three novels are *The Bird Saviors* (2012), *Goodnight Texas* (2006), and *The Fire Eaters* (1994), and his story collections are *The Lousy Adult* (2013) and *The White Tattoo* (2002).

As a full-time student at University of Pittsburgh at Greensburg, **Nicole Cortino** is completing her Bachelor's, double majoring in Psychology and Creative Professional Writing with a Criminal Justice Minor.

Nicole is a reporter for her university's newspaper and the president of the Creative Writing Club. Her future plans consist of becoming a part of a multidisciplinary child protective team and earning a psychology doctorate degree. She spends most of her time with her younger sister bike riding and playing with their cats.

Riley Danvers graduated in 2016 with her A.S. in English and in 2018 with her B.A. in English Literature and Writing. Her fiction and non-fiction have been published in more than twenty-five online and printed literary journals and anthologies. Her poetry has been published in *Z Publishing House*, *Silkworm*, and *Clackamas Literary Review*, and is forthcoming in *Other Worldly Women Press*. Riley is currently pursuing her M.F.A. in Creative Writing at the Pacific Northwest College of Art.

Hannah Davis (she/her) is an aspiring poet and short story writer. She is a recent graduate of Clackamas Community College with an Associates of Science in English degree and a current student of Portland State University working toward a BFA degree. She is a creative writing major with the goals of becoming a published writer. She has a few publications under her belt including two poems that were published in her high school's literary review, *The Laureate*.

Susanne Davis is the author of a linked short story collection, *The Appointed Hour*, published by Cornerstone Press and in its 2nd printing. Her stories have been published in *American Short Fiction*, *Notre Dame Review*, *St. Petersburg Literary Review*, and numerous others. She teaches creative writing at Hope College and has just completed a novel about two siblings trying to find their way home in a divided

America. "The Dacha" was part of the first draft but didn't fit into the novel in the end.

Adam Day is the author of *Left-Handed Wolf* (LSU Press, 2020), and of *Model of a City in Civil War* (Sarabande Books), and the recipient of a Poetry Society of America Chapbook Fellowship for *Badger, Apocrypha*, and of a PEN Award. He is the editor of the forthcoming anthology, *Divine Orphans of the Poetic Project*, from 1913 Press, and his work has appeared in the *Prism International, American Poetry Review, The Maynard, Boston Review, Poetry Ireland, London Magazine, Kenyon Review, Iowa Review*, and elsewhere. He is the publisher of *Action, Spectacle*.

Linda Drach works on projects to end health disparities, grows spinach and sunflowers, and is actively involved in community writing through the nonprofit Write Around Portland. Her poetry has been published in the *Timberline Review, Hole in the Head Review*, and *VoiceCatcher*.

Bernard W. Duffy is a playwright. He lives in the woods of the Pacific Northwest in an RV.

Meli Broderick Eaton's work has appeared in numerous publications, including *Crosswinds Poetry Journal, Smartish Pace, Writer's Digest, Flying South*, and *The Source Weekly*. She won first place for new poets in the Oregon Poetry Association contest, followed shortly by the Sixfold Poetry Prize. Her poems have also recently been named runner-up for the Erskine J. Poetry Prize, and finalist for both the 49th Parallel Award and the poetry award in the Tucson Festival of Books.

Her short fiction has been a finalist for the New Millennium Prize and appeared as an honorable mention entry in Tulip Tree Publication's anthology. Her education started with Mary Oliver at Sweet Briar College and is finishing with an MFA through Lindenwood University. She lives with her family in the high desert of Oregon.

Andrew Rader Hanson is a native of Florida, and he took an interest in writing and literature and recently completed studies at UCL in London. He now lives in Miami, where among other things he works at a law firm, fishes on weekends, enjoys photography, lifts weights, and voraciously reads history, philosophy, and poetry. He has recently been accepted by *Broadkill Review, Bookends Review, Ekphrastic Review, Birmingham Arts, Thirty West,* and more.

William Heath has published two chapbooks, *Night Moves in Ohio* and *Leaving Seville*; a book of poems, *The Walking Man*; three novels: *The Children Bob Moses Led, Devil Dancer,* and *Blacksnake's Path*; an award-winning work of history, *Wiliam Wells and the Struggle for the Old Northwest*; and a collection of interviews, *Conversations with Robert Stone.*

Over four dozen of **Madronna Holden's** poems have appeared in 21 journals in a little over two years. In addition to appearing in a recent issue of *Clackamas Literary Review,* her work has appeared in *Equinox Poetry and Prose, The Bitter Oleander, The Cold Mountain Review, Puerto del Sol, The Slippery Elm Literary Journal,* and elsewhere. Her chapbook, *The Goddess of Glass Mountains,* is forthcoming from Finishing Line Press.

Wynne Hungerford's work has appeared in *Epoch, Subtropics, Blackbird, The Brooklyn Review, Iron Horse Literary Review, American Literary Review, The Normal School, The Whitefish Review,* and *SmokeLong Quarterly,* among other places. She received her MFA from the University of Florida.

Marc Jampole wrote *Music from Words* (Bellday Books, 2007) and *Cubist States of Mind/Not the Cruelest Month* (Poet's Haven Press, 2017). Owl Canyon Press will be publishing his novel, *The Brothers Silver,* in 2021. His poems and short stories have appeared in many journals and anthologies. About 1,800 freelance articles he has written have been published. A former television reporter and public relations executive, Marc writes the OpEdge blog, which appears on the websites of three national publications. He is past president of the board of *Jewish Currents,* a national magazine of politics and arts.

M. Jennings lives on the Oregon coast where she is revising two allegorical literary novels. Her short stories, creative nonfiction, and poetry have appeared in *Hotel Amerika, Fiction Southeast, Oyster River Pages,* and *Crab Orchard Review,* among others.

Brook Johnson is a high school student who has been working on her craft for the last seven years. She enjoys inspiration from daily experience and the freedom to make art that captures that experience.

Jeffrey Kingman lives by the Napa River in Vallejo, California. His poetry collection, *Beyond That Hill I Gather,* will be published by Finishing Line Press in May of 2021. His poetry chapbook, *On A Road,* was published by Finishing Line Press in December of 2019. He is the winner of the Red Berry Editions 2015 Broadside Contest, the winner of the 2018 Eyelands Book Award (Greece) for an unpublished poetry book, a finalist in the 2018 Hillary Gravendyk Prize poetry book competition, and he received honorable mention in the 2017 Quercus Review Press Fall Poetry Book Award. He has been published in *PANK*, *Crack the Spine*, *Squaw Valley Review*, *Visitant*, and others. Jeff has a Master's degree in Music Composition and has been playing drums in rock bands most of his life.

Robert Krut is the author of *The Now Dark Sky, Setting Us All on Fire* (Codhill/SUNY Press, 2019), which received the Codhill Poetry Award, *This Is the Ocean* (Bona Fide Books, 2013), and *The Spider Sermons* (BlazeVox, 2009). He lives in Los Angeles, and teaches at the University of California, Santa Barbara.

Jeffrey Letterly is a composer and multi-disciplined performer. He was born and raised in the heartland of the Midwest and now resides in Syracuse, NY. His poetry won 3rd place and an honorable mention in the 2020 Atticus Review Poetry Contest and can also be found in a previous issue of *Clackamas Literary Review*.

Mary Makofske's latest books are *World Enough, and Time* (Kelsay, 2017) and *Traction* (Ashland, 2011), winner of the Richard Snyder Prize. Her poems have appeared recently in *The American Journal of Poetry*, *The MacGuffin*, *Spillway*, *Southern Poetry Review*, *Bryant Literary Review*, *The Stillwater Review*, and *Crosswinds*, as well as in nineteen anthologies. In 2017 she received the Atlanta Review International Poetry Prize and the New Millennium Poetry Prize. She is a retired English professor who lives in New York's Hudson Valley.

Steven Mayer, a retired professor, and his wife, Linda, live on Oregon's North Coast. Steven authored *Finding Heart* (2012) and *Finding More Heart* (2018). Steven and Linda coauthored *Retire Smart* (2020).

Melissa McKinstry lives and writes in San Diego where she mothers her disabled adult child, curates a neighborhood poet tree, and assists with translation of Yiddish literature. She is working on her thesis in the Pacific University MFA program. Her work has appeared in *The Seattle Review*, *San Diego Poetry Annual*, and earned honorable mention for the 2020 Steve Kowit Poetry Prize.

Colton Merris was a finalist in the Oregon Writer's Colony Fiction contest. He has had poetry published in *Pathos Literary Magazine* and fiction published in *Oregon City Digest*. He lives in Portland, Oregon.

After 37 years of teaching English at Roseville High School, **Cecil Morris** has turned his attention to writing poetry. He has poems appearing in 2*River View*, *Cobalt Review*, *Ekphrastic Review*, *Midwest Quarterly*, and *Poem*. He enjoys the work of Sharon Olds, Billy Collins, Tony Hoagland, Morgan Parker, and torrin a. greathouse among others.

Scott F. Parker is the author of *Being on the Oregon Coast* and *A Way Home: Oregon Essays*, as well a the editor of *Conversations with Joan Didion*, among other books. He teaches writing at Montana State University.

Ricardo Pau-Llosa's eighth book of poems, *The Turning* (2018), is from his longtime publisher, Carnegie Mellon U Press. Aside from various anthologies, his poems have also appeared in *Ambit, American Journal of Poetry, American Poetry Review, Arion, Birmingham Poetry Review, Blackbird, Bombay Review, Boston Review, Burnside, december, The Fiddlehead, Hudson Review, Ilanot Review, Island, Kenyon Review, Manoa, New England Review, Ploughshares, Plume, PN Review, Poetry, Prism, Quadrant, Southern Review, Stand, Virginia Quarterly Review,* and *Volt,* among other journals.

Barry Peters and his wife, the writer Maureen Sherbondy, live in Durham, NC. He teaches in Raleigh. Publications include *The American Journal of Poetry, Best New Poets, New Ohio Review, Poetry East, Rattle,* and *The Southampton Review.*

Daniel Pié, 70, is retired. He was a daily newspaper journalist for 44-plus years, the final 30 as a copy editor at *The Arizona Republic,* in Phoenix.

Geoff Polk is a writer, teacher, and musician living in Cleveland. He attended Berklee College of Music and has an MA in creative writing from Cleveland State University. He was editor of *Whiskey Island.* Geoff's poems and fiction have appeared in *Brilliant Corners, Cobalt Review, Loud Coffee Press,* and elsewhere. Nonfiction publications include articles on jazz and literature and interviews of David Foster Wallace and Ken Kesey.

Vivienne Popperl lives in Portland, Oregon. She finds nourishment and hope in nature and poetry. Her work has appeared in several publications including *Willawaw Journal, Cirque, Clackamas Literary Review,* and *The Timberline Review.*

Bruce Pratt is an award-winning novelist, short story writer, poet, and playwright. He is the author of the novel *The Serpents of Blissfull* from Mountain State Press, the poetry collection *Boreal* from Antrim House Books, *The Trash Detail: Stories from New Rivers Press*, and the poetry chapbook *Forms and Shades* from Clare Songbirds Publishing. His fiction, poetry, drama, and essays have appeared in more than fifty magazines, reviews, and journals across the United States, and in Canada, Ireland, and Wales. He is the editor of *American Fiction*.

Levi Rogers is a Colorado native, writer, and former coffee roaster currently based in the land of the Chinook and Multnomah people. He has an MFA in Creative Nonfiction from Antioch University Los Angeles and a Bachelors of English from the University of Utah. He's published essays, poetry, fiction, and reviews in *Entropy, Sojourners, Lunch Ticket, Drunk Monkeys, Akashic Books, Revolv Magazine, Hoot, A Deeper Story, StandArt, Freshcup, Roast Magazine*, and *Devour Magazine*. His debut novel, *Utah! A Novel* is forthcoming from Atmosphere Press on April 20th, 2021. Rogers has attended residencies at the Lighthouse Writer's Workshop in 2020, the Tin House Summer Workshop in 2018, and the Writer's Hotel Conference in 2017. He has read at the Utah Arts Festival and served on Antioch University's literary journal, *Lunch Ticket*. He owns and runs a coffee roasting company, La Barba Coffee, in Salt Lake City, Utah, where he lived for the last eight years before moving to Portland, Oregon, where he lives with his wife and two daughters.

Mary Rohrer-Dann is the author of *Taking the Long Way Home*, (Kelsay Books, 2021) and *La Scaffetta: Poems from the Foundling*

Drawer (Tempest Productions, Inc.) She is a two-time Pushcart nominee, with stories and poems in *Flash Fiction Magazine, Boston Literary Magazine, Third Wednesday, MacQueen's Quinterly*, and other venues. Two verse play projects, *La Scaffetta* and *Accidents of Being*, were staged by Tempest Productions, Inc.

Karen Sandberg lives and writes in Minneapolis, MN. She has been published in *Freshwater Journal, Vita Brevis*, and *Main Street Rag*, to name a few. During this pandemic, she hikes with her partner, Ed, in the multitude of beautiful parks in the Mpls metro area.

Mark Simpson is the author of *Fat Chance* (Finishing Line Press). Recent work has appeared in *Sleet* (Pushcart Prize nominee), *Columbia Journal* (Online), *Third Wednesday*, and *Apeiron Review*. He lives on Whidbey Island, Washington, where he farms several acres of once-forest, raising what the climate and land allow. He has a calendar, and as each day passes, he places a careful X in the small white square of yesterday.

Geo. Staley is retired from teaching at Portland Community College. His poetry has appeared in *Chest, Four Quarters, Loonfeather, New Mexico Humanities Review, Blue Mountain Review, Fireweed, Freshwater, Santa Fe Literary Review*, and others. He has a short story in a recent issue of *Plainsongs*.

Jeanine Stevens is the author of *Limberlost and Inheritor* (Future Cycle Press). Her first poetry collection, *Sailing on Milkweed*, was published by Cherry Grove Collections. She is winner of the MacGuffin Poet Hunt, The Stockton Arts Commission Award, The Ekphrasis Prize, and WOMR Cape Cod Community Radio National Poetry Award. *Brief Immensity* won the Finishing Line Press Open Chapbook Award. Jeanine recently received her sixth Pushcart Nomination. She participated in Literary Lectures sponsored by Poets and Writers. Work has appeared in *North Dakota Review, Pearl, Stoneboat, Rosebud, Chiron Review,* and *Evansville Review.* Jeanine studied poetry at U.C. Davis, earned her M.A. at CSU Sacramento, and has a doctorate in Education. She is also a collage artist and has exhibited her work in various art galleries. Jeanine is Professor Emerita at American River College. Raised in Indiana, she now divides her time between Sacramento and Lake Tahoe.

Robert Stone was born in Wolverhampton in the UK. He works in a press cuttings agency in London. Before that he was a teacher and then foreman of a London Underground station. He has two children and lives with his partner in Ipswich. He has had stories published in *Stand, Panurge, The Write Launch, Eclectica, Confingo, Here Comes Everyone, Punt Volat, The Decadent Review, Heirlock, The Pearl River Quarterly,* and *Wraparound South.* He has had a story published in Nicholas Royle's Nightjar chapbook series. Micro stories have been published by Palm-Sized Press, *5x5, Star 82, The Ocotillo Review, deathcap,* and *Clover & White.* Longer stories will soon come out in *The Cabinet of Heed, The Wisconsin Review, 3:AM,* and *The Main Street Rag.* A story appeared in Salt's *Best British Stories* 2020 volume.

Stephanie Striffler recently retired after decades of public service as a lawyer for the people of Oregon. Her work has appeared in publications including *Calyx, Voicecatcher, Timberline Review,* and *Persim-*

mon Tree. She has a passion for birds; to date, she and her husband have recorded 55 bird species in their Portland yard.

Anannya Uberoi is a full-time software engineer and part-time tea connoisseur based in Madrid. She is poetry editor at *The Bookends Review*, the winner of the 6th Singapore Poetry Contest, and a Pushcart Prize nominee. Her work has appeared in *The Bangalore Review*, *The Birmingham Arts Journal*, and *The New York Public Library Magazine.*

Peter Vertacnik's poems and translations have appeared in *The Hopkins Review*, *Literary Matters*, *Poet Lore*, *Valparaiso Poetry Review*, and *Water-Stone Review*, among others. A finalist for the 2021 Donald Justice Poetry Prize, he currently attends the MFA program at The University of Florida.

John Walser's poems have appeared in numerous journals, including *Spillway*, *Mantis*, *the Normal School*, *Water-Stone*, *december magazine*, and *Lumina*. His manuscript *Edgewood Orchard Galleries* has been a finalist for the Autumn House Press Prize (2016) and the Ballard Spahr Prize (2020), as well as a semifinalist for both the Philip Levine Prize (2016 and 2017) and the Crab Orchard Series First Book Award (2017 and 2018). An English professor at Marian University-Wisconsin, John is a four-time semifinalist for the Neruda Prize.

Francis Walsh is a writer from coastal Maine, where they share an apartment with one human, two rabbits, and a spider plant. Their work appears or is forthcoming in *Brevity*, *East by Northeast*, and the *Gateway Review.*

Alanna Weissman is a writer, reporter, and editor from New York City. Her work across genres has appeared in *The New York Times*, *The Guardian*, *San Francisco Chronicle*, *Barely South Review*, *Salon*, *Entropy*, and elsewhere. She is currently an MFA candidate at New York University, where she edits the *Washington Square Review*, and she also holds an MS from Columbia Journalism School and a BA in creative writing and studio art from Colgate University.

Darlene Young published her first collection, *Homespun and Angel Feathers* (BCC Press) in 2019. She teaches creative writing at Brigham Young University, and has served as poetry editor for *Dialogue Journal* and *Segullah*. Her work has been noted in *Best American Essays* and nominated for Pushcart prizes. She lives in South Jordan, Utah with her husband and sons.

The *Clackamas Literary Review* is typeset in Sabon LT Std, an old-style serif designed by Jan Tschichold, and in Optima, a humanistic sans-serif designed by Hermann Zapf, and printed on 50 lb. creme paper. Editing and design done by English Department students and faculty at Clackamas Community College, in Oregon City, Oregon.

Visit

CLR
CLACKAMAS LITERARY REVIEW

clackamasliteraryreview.org
clackamasliteraryreview.submittable.com
facebook.com/clackamasliteraryreview
@clackamaslitrev

Contact
clr@clackamas.edu

CLACKAMAS LITERARY REVIEW

the finest writing for the best readers

Clackamas Literary Review has been committed to publishing quality writing from around the world since 1997. Use the form below or visit us on Submittable to receive the latest and forthcoming issues.

Clackamas Literary Review

_____	1 year	$12
_____	2 years	$22
_____	3 years	$32

Name _____

Address _____

City / State / Zip _____

Email _____

Send this form and check or money order to:

Clackamas Literary Review
English Department
Clackamas Community College
19600 Molalla Avenue
Oregon City, Oregon 97045